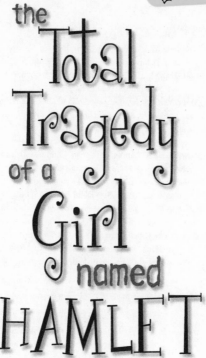

the
Total
Tragedy
of a
Girl
named
HAMLET

Erin Dionne

Dial Books for Young Readers

An imprint of Penguin Group (USA) Inc.

DIAL BOOKS FOR YOUNG READERS
A division of Penguin Young Readers Group
Published by The Penguin Group
Penguin Group (USA) Inc., 375 Hudson Street, New York, NY 10014, U.S.A.
Penguin Group (Canada), 90 Eglinton Avenue East, Suite 700, Toronto, Ontario, Canada
M4P 2Y3 (a division of Pearson Penguin Canada Inc.)
Penguin Books Ltd, 80 Strand, London WC2R ORL, England
Penguin Ireland, 25 St. Stephen's Green, Dublin 2, Ireland
(a division of Penguin Books Ltd)
Penguin Group (Australia), 250 Camberwell Road, Camberwell, Victoria 3124, Australia
(a division of Pearson Australia Group Pty Ltd)
Penguin Books India Pvt Ltd, 11 Community Centre,
Panchsheel Park, New Delhi - 110 017, India
Penguin Group (NZ), 67 Apollo Drive, Rosedale, North Shore 0632,
New Zealand (a division of Pearson New Zealand Ltd)
Penguin Books (South Africa) (Pty) Ltd, 24 Sturdee Avenue,
Rosebank, Johannesburg 2196, South Africa
Penguin Books Ltd, Registered Offices: 80 Strand,
London WC2R ORL, England

The publisher does not have any control over and does not assume any responsibility
for author or third-party websites or their content.

Book design by Jasmin Rubero
Text set in Bodoni Old Face

Printed in the U.S.A.
1 3 5 7 9 10 8 6 4 2

Library of Congress Cataloging-in-Publication Data
Dionne, Erin, date.
The total tragedy of a girl named Hamlet / by Erin Dionne.
p.   cm.
Summary: Hamlet's attempts to be a "normal" eighth grader become
increasingly difficult when her genius seven-year-old sister and her
eccentric Shakespeare scholar parents both begin to attend her school.
ISBN 978-0-8037-3535-4
[1. Sisters—Fiction. 2. Interpersonal relations—Fiction.
3. Self-confidence—Fiction. 4. Middle schools—Fiction.
5. Schools—Fiction. 6. Shakespeare, William, 1564–1616—Fiction.] I. Title.
PZ7.D6216To 2010
[Fic]—dc22
2009023059

For Mom, Dad, and Lindsay, who have always
encouraged me to follow my passion

TABLE OF CONTENTS

the
Total
Tragedy
of a
Girl
named
HAMLET

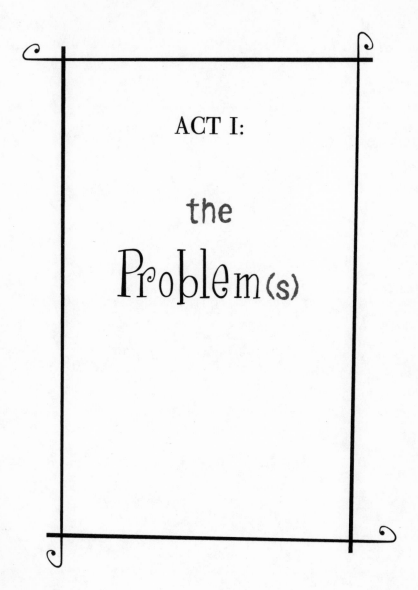

ACT I:

the

Problem(s)

I hadn't figured out a way to stop time, join the circus, or make myself invisible. I hadn't been able to contract a serious (but not life-threatening) illness, change my identity, or get into the witness protection program. I hadn't even been able to talk my mother into staying home or waiting in the car.

Instead, I had to follow Mom—dressed like an Elizabethan-era superhero with purple velvet cloak billowing and bells a'tinkling—down the hall. I had to escort my sister to the main office. I had to act like this was normal.

I had to start eighth grade.

Every seventh and eighth grader in the main hall watched us like we were a parade: They stopped spinning locker dials and cut off "how was your summer" conversations. The already confused sixth graders just stood and stared. I couldn't blame them. I mean, how often do a woman dressed in full Shakespearean regalia, a seven-year-old, and a humiliated eighth grader traipse through the middle of a junior high school on the first day of classes?

Exactly.

So I kept my eyes glued to the floor a few feet in front of me, my face neutral, stayed as far back from them as I could . . . and tried not to see the gaping mouths or hear the giggles and murmurs that filled in behind us as we passed. Just as we reached the main office, out of the corner of my eye, I saw my two least favorite people: Saber Greene and Mauri Lee, nudging each other. Ugh.

Mom pushed the office door open and went in, followed by my sister. I scooted in last, which at least cut off my view of the not-so-dynamic duo, and tried to pull the heavy, slow-moving door closed.

"Good will to you." It was Mom's standard greeting.

Mrs. Pearl, the school secretary, didn't even blink at Mom's billowy poet blouse, cloak, severe bun, or teeny round reading glasses. To her, I'm sure my mother's seventeenth-century attire was the height of style. No one had ever seen the secretary leave the office. For all we knew, she *could* have been there since the 1600s.

"Good morning and welcome back! This must be our new student," Mrs. Pearl chirped. She leaned over the half wall surrounding her desk to get a glimpse of my sister, who was barely tall enough to see over it. Dezzie gave her a tight smile.

Our secretary sat down and pecked at the keys on her computer, one finger at a time. "Now, let me see . . . it's Kennedy, right?"

My mother nodded. "*Desdemona* Kennedy."

I shifted from foot to foot, feeling anxiety coil in my belly. This was *not* the way eighth grade was supposed to start. The computer churned and gurgled.

"Here you are! What a pretty name! Unique, like your sister's." Mrs. Pearl scanned the screen. "Schedule . . . schedule . . . Here we go!" The first bell rang.

"Is that the late bell?" Mom asked as the buzzing died down. She twirled the tassels on her cloak and picked at the hem. Dezzie rocked back and forth, from heel to toe, while we waited. I stuffed my hands into the pockets of my capris and clenched my fists.

"Three-minute warning," Mrs. Pearl explained. My mouth went as dry as the top of her desk. This was actually happening. Would the freeze-frame scene in the hall be repeated every day? "Then we ring the late bell."

"Well, better three hours too soon than a minute too late," Mom replied, using one of her favorite Shakespeare quotes. I cringed.

Mrs. Pearl nodded. Her printer whirred to life. "Now, Desdemona," she said, plucking the paper off the tray, "these are your classes. I see that your day ends after fourth period?"

"Yes," Mom said. "That's when she'll go home to work on her college curriculum." She placed a hand on my sister's shoulder.

"And Hamlet will escort her to each room, or should

3

I assign a student helper to do that?" Mrs. Pearl asked. The three pairs of eyes—Mom's, Dezzie's, and Mrs. Pearl's—swung in my direction. I swallowed hard, then nodded.

Like it or not, my seven-year-old sister was in eighth grade with me.

This is how it happened:

The Scene: *Two weeks before school begins. Mom, Dad, and me in the living room. Gold velvet drapes hang to the floor, heavy dark furniture lines the perimeter of the room. It's clear that this space isn't used much. Mom and Dad, seated on the sofa—what they call the "settee." Me, in the chair across from them—what I call the "hot seat."*

Mom (grinning): We have something special
      to tell you!

Me (knowing that "special conversations" +
      living room = not good): . . . ?

Mom: We have been told that Desdemona
      needs some additional coursework before
      taking her next step. And we think it would
      be perfect if she did that work with *you.*

Me (sure I hadn't heard right): With *me?* At
      HoHo?

They nod.

4

Dad: She needs the social experience. She's too young for high school.

Me (shocked): She's too young for eighth grade too!

Mom and Dad exchange glances.

Me (trying to regain control): She'll be bored. The work's too easy for her. Teachers won't know what to do with her.

Mom (frowning): She is going to follow her special academic curriculum in the after- noons, but will be taking regular fine art and music classes in the morning at How- ard Hoffer. The decision has been made.

From that point on, there was no changing their minds. See, Dezzie's a genius. Certifiable. Her IQ is off the charts—she scored a 210 on some test when she was only two years old. Whatever that number means, it was high enough for two newspapers and a magazine to write about her. At four, Dezzie ripped through the assigned reading for my parents' courses before Thanksgiving. She could barely hold a pencil, so she dictated assignments into a mini voice recorder. Seriously.

Mom and Dad homeschooled her, let her sit in on the classes they teach at Chestnut College outside of Boston, and gave her every "academic opportunity" they could.

So by the time she was five, she'd started her "immersion projects." That's her name for them. My name is "nutty obsessions." A nutty obsession project starts when something catches her curiosity—something she reads about, something on the news, in a museum, whatever—and then she learns everything there is to know about it. So far, she's "immersed herself" in Chinese political history, the Black Plague and its effect on medieval Europe, Olympic curling, Greek drama, and ornithology (the geektastic study of *birds*). She was supposed to be going to college full-time this year, but since she hadn't taken any art or music, Chestnut College wouldn't let her declare a major until she held a paintbrush or sang a song. Howard Hoffer Junior High to the rescue.

And Hamlet Kennedy to the land of embarrassment.

Mrs. Pearl passed Dezzie's schedule to my mom.

"So, Desdemona will be in Mr. Symphony's homeroom, with her sister," Mrs. Pearl said. By the way her eyes jumped from my mom to Dezzie, it was clear that she didn't know who she should be talking to. Behind me, the door kept opening as other kids came in to deal with first-day problems. I gazed at a spot over Mrs. Pearl's desk and hoped that no other eighth graders were in the room.

Don't get me wrong, I love my sister. And we actually get along, mostly because we don't have much in common. There's no reason for us to bug each other. I mean,

6

really—what am I going to do, steal her math textbooks? Hide her pipettes?

But now we'd have one major thing in common. Something that I never had to share with her: school. A whole year's worth—starting today.

"Then there's music appreciation. After that, you'll both go to Art IIB, then you'll go to choir and the TLC room." She glanced at my mother apologetically. "We scheduled the music classes close together, so we thought TLC would be the best place for Desdemona to wait until you can pick her up at lunchtime." Mom had two morning classes this fall, and Dezzie was too young to walk home on her own.

"TLC? What's that?" Dezzie asked. It was the first time she'd said anything since we'd left the house, and her pipsqueak-y voice snapped me out of my wishing-hoping-praying.

TLC was The Learning Center, a place where kids went to get extra help on their work.

"Well, she doesn't need any extra help," my mother said. I had to agree with her.

"We thought Desdemona could use the library and read during that period," said Mrs. Pearl.

I wanted to shake my head, or snort, or roll my eyes at the thought of my super-smart sister in our junior high library. She'd probably read half the books in there already. She'd kill the other half in a week.

7

"I could do my calculus homework," Dezzie suggested.

"Lovely idea!" chirped Mrs. Pearl. My mother beamed.

Where was that serious (but not life-threatening) illness when you needed it?

~ii~

I don't remember if Mrs. Pearl said anything more, or if Mom did anything else weird or Renaissance-y in the office. Once Dezzie's schedule was set, my situation sunk in. My fingertips went cold and my stomach fizzed. Eighth grade was supposed to be me scoring a good lunch table with my friends, working on whatever the class project would be, and not getting picked on by older kids. It was supposed to be us showing the sixth graders where their classes were—and sometimes pointing them in the wrong direction—not me towing around a child brainiac.

Mom led us from the office as though it was the final stretch of the parade. After seeing the backlog of kids who had been waiting behind us, that's what it felt like too. The late bell had buzzed; the halls were empty.

"Huzzah!" Mom exclaimed—it's like a Renaissance cheerleader word. "It is your first day of school. I am so proud." She bent down to Dezzie's level to give her a kiss, then she turned to me.

This was nothing to cheer about. I pulled away as she swooped in, getting a tassel across the nose but no mom-smooch. Even though everyone was in class, and no one was around to see me, being wrapped in her purple velvet drapery in the middle of school? No way. She straightened and sighed. Then she peered over her glasses at me.

"We're late already," I pointed out, feeling a twinge of guilt at my evasive maneuver.

Mom's eyes darkened. "Hamlet, you know how I feel about the use of contractions."

"Commoner's speech," I muttered. Mom nodded.

Another peck on Dezzie's cheek, and she spun to leave, cloak flowing, bells chiming.

I forced my feet to move in the opposite direction, toward Mr. Symphony's homeroom and the disaster that was going to be this school year. Dezzie's quick steps tapped behind me.

"I am intrigued by the type of sociological observation I will have the opportunity to interpret while here," Dezzie said as we made our way to the second level. "I know I am in need of social development, but I am not sure how to behave as part of such a large group of pre-adolescents."

"Is this your way of saying that you're nervous?" I asked, surprised. It never occurred to me that always-together Dezzie would be nervous about anything. We'd reached the landing.

"A little," Dezzie admitted. "And slightly excited. It is, after all, my first day of school. Have you any suggestions as to how I should approach my days here?"

Her words jolted me from my own worries. She stood, new backpack that was nearly as large as she was slung over her shoulder, wearing a purple trapeze shirt and black leggings. Dark curly hair fluffed around her round face and big gray eyes. Mom and Dad said my eyes were the same color as hers when I was a baby, but they'd settled into a dark blue. We have the same curls, though, and Mom's wide smile—there's no denying we're related. Dezzie seemed ready for second grade, not eighth. And definitely not college. What could I possibly tell her? After all, *she* was the one who helped *me* decipher word problems when I was in fifth grade and she was four.

But then it occurred to me:

Living in my family, I understand there's a lot that I *don't* know. And I'm okay with that, mostly. Dezzie's major educational moments take place outside of my "interaction sphere" with the family, to quote my mom. But this, this was different. Maybe this was the way to save my last year of junior high. Or at least try to.

"Try to fit in," I offered, and continued up the stairs. "Don't yell huzzah, or use Shakespeare quotes when you talk to people. And don't talk about school unless someone asks you a specific question about it."

She nodded. "I can do that. Can you do me a favor?"

Besides the one I was doing already? But I didn't say that out loud. I nodded, instead. "Sure."

"Please don't tell anyone how old I am. I don't want to make people uncomfortable."

I hated to break it to her, but it was obvious that she fit in here about as well as a chicken in a post office.

"Okay. Sure," I responded. We'd arrived at homeroom.

The door to room 251 was closed. I faked a smile for Dezzie—and myself—took a deep breath, and pushed it open. Eighteen pairs of eyes turned in our direction.

Mr. Symphony, wearing the same tweed blazer he'd worn every day for the two years I'd been at HoHo, stood at the front of the room holding his attendance list. Had his comb-over moved closer to his left ear since last spring? Possibly.

"Ms. Kennedy," he said. "Not an auspicious start to the year." Someone in the back of the room snickered. I wanted to melt into the floor.

"Sorry, Mr. S.," I responded, trying to be casual. "I have a pass." I held it out to him. He took it from me and barely glanced at it.

"And your friend?"

Dezzie curtsied. "Desdemona Kennedy, sir. Newly matriculated."

Yep. She curtsied.

A wave of laughter crashed in my ears. I guess I should have been more specific with my "try to fit in" instructions.

Mr. S. raised an eyebrow. The laughter stopped. Somehow, that made it worse. Dezzie just stood there, completely unbothered. I wanted a trapdoor to fall through—exit stage, Hamlet!

"She's my sister." My dry throat rasped against the words. Everyone was still staring. I tried hard to focus on Mr. Symphony's face and not the expressions of my classmates. A murmur went through the room.

Mr. S. turned to Dezzie. "I heard you might be joining us this term. We're glad to have you here." Back to me. "You and your sister may take your seats now. See that you aren't late again."

Of course our desks were in the middle of the room. I forced myself to pass Nirmal Grover's and Mark Sloughman's front-row grins and hoped Dezzie wouldn't make any other classic Renaissance moves. I wished one of my good friends was in my homeroom, then immediately changed my mind—with no friend-witnesses, it'd be easier to forget that this ever happened.

I slid into my seat, still hearing the echo of laughter in my ears, and saw the next problem: The desks were way too tall for Dezzie. Her feet didn't touch the floor and the top was too high for her to rest her arms on it. Thankfully, instead of saying anything, she just folded her hands in her lap and sat as straight as a ruler. It didn't stop the stares and whispers that floated around us. But that's her thing—most of the time Dezzie's like a mini adult. She calls it "taking the long view" in life—she says "small inconveniences" don't really matter in the big picture. Clearly, my picture's a lot smaller than hers.

Finally, Mr. Symphony went back to the morning announcements and standard homeroom lecture. I tuned him out, reactivated my breathing, and scanned the class. Tense and edgy, I felt more like I had on my first day of sixth grade than I should have on my first day of eighth.

Something—the top of a pencil?—poked between my shoulder blades. I ignored it. It poked again. I tried to remember who was behind me . . . Julie Kennelly? Not your typical pencil-poker. I hunched forward; another tap. This time it was followed by a hiss.

"*Here.*"

A note.

I stretched my arms behind me, my eyes on the back of Dezzie's head and a neutral expression on my face. The folded slip of paper slid into my palm.

I brought my hands to the top of the desk and faked an itch on my leg to unfold the note off Mr. S.'s radar. It read:

Oink you glad to be back at school? I'm sure glad you are! Below the words was a smiling inked pig face wearing a bow with an "oink" balloon coming out of its mouth.

My hands went cold and my neck prickled. That hadn't taken long.

Not like the nicknames and pig jokes were anything new. See, Mom and Dad are Shakespeare scholars (that purple cloak gave it away, right?). Mom's into the tragedies and histories, Dad teaches the sonnets and comedies. Together, they're a collection of "if thous, then thees."

When they had me, *Hamlet* was the play they both liked the best . . . and they thought naming me Ophelia, after Hamlet's suicidal girlfriend, would be too morbid. So I ended up with not just any boy's name, but the name of a tragic Denmarkian prince who spoke to skulls and had a thing for his mother. So I'm a little touchy about it. Unsurprisingly, Dezzie thinks her name is cool. It's from another play, *Othello.* She's named for Othello's wife, who is killed in a jealous rage . . . yet *that* wasn't too weird for my parents. Go figure.

I struggled against the urge to scan the room to see if the note writer would give him- or herself away. I didn't want to give anyone the satisfaction of seeing my irritation. Or fear. This was the first anonymous note I'd ever received, and I didn't know what to make of it. I focused on Dezzie's thick mop of curls and pretended that this wasn't happening.

The bell rang, signaling the end of homeroom and the switch to first period. Dezzie had music appreciation. I hadn't even glanced at my own schedule.

History, Mr. Hoffstedder, room 306. Dezzie's class would be in the music hall on the opposite side of the building, down a floor. I'd have to add super speed to my wish list today if I was going to make it to my class in time.

"Let's go," I said to her. She'd slid out of her seat and

was checking out the posters of mathematicians on Mr. Symphony's walls. "I'll take you to your classes for a few days, so you know where to go. Once you learn where they are, you can go by yourself."

We hoisted our backpacks and left the classroom. Kids rushed by and called to one another; sixth graders clutched maps and schedules, trying to keep an eye on room numbers as they wandered. It was barely controlled chaos. I'd long since gotten used to it, but seeing it through Dezzie's eyes, it seemed noisy and scary. And even when she learned where those classes were, I doubted I could let her walk the halls alone. She was just too small. Her head came up to most of the other kids' shoulders, and a couple of them bumped into her because they were busy looking for friends and classrooms instead of extra-short students. I glanced down. My sister's eyebrows were knitted together in a tight line.

"Are you okay?" I raised my voice above slamming lockers and hoots and yells. She nodded.

"It is louder than I thought," was all she said.

We made it to the music hall just as the first bell rang, and I introduced her to Ms. Applebaum, the choir director. No curtsy this time—I'd warned Dezzie on our walk.

As I bolted up to the third floor, the words of the note came back to me:

Oink you glad to be back at school?

Pigs-a-tively not.

16

I slid into Mr. Hoffstedder's room just as the tardy bell buzzed.

My best friend, Ty, and our other friend Ely—who'd followed through on his promise to start dreadlocks over the summer and had sprouted little nubs all over his head—saved me a seat close to the door. I plopped into it, trying to catch my breath.

Ty and I had been best friends almost from birth. His mother took my mother's *Othello* adult education class when we were babies, and they became friends. For a few summers, when Chestnut College was on vacation, my parents even watched Ty when his mom was at work. At the front of the room, Mr. Hoffstedder began taking attendance.

"How's it going with Short and Smart?" Ty whispered. I shrugged. He and I had spent the two weeks before school started trying to figure out what would happen once Dezzie was at HoHo.

The Scene: *Before school begins. Ty and I sit at the back table at the Chilly Spoon, the local ice cream shop. Black* *and pink checkered cups, filled with chocolate frappe (Ty) and strawberry frappe (me), in front of us.*

Me: Guess who's going to be in our class this fall?

Ty (scrunching up his face): All the usual people?

Me: Yeah. And *(takes a deep breath)* Dezzie.

Ty: Dezzie? Come off it. Who, really?

He takes a sip of his frappe. I explain the situation.

Ty: Dezzie's going to HoHo . . . whoa.

Plunks his drink onto the table.

Ty: That's awesome!

Me: So *not* awesome. My parents will be everywhere. You know how they get. They need to make sure that she's getting every academic experience, all the time. It'll be horrible.

Ty (after a minute): You're right. This could be very bad.

I nod.

Ty: So bad, it's probably going to ruin your life.

I nod again.

Ty (seriously): Then we better get more ice cream now, before you become a complete social outcast and we can't be friends anymore.

I throw a straw wrapper at him.

At the time, I knew he was kidding. But I couldn't help but wonder if his words would end up coming true. Having Mom at school this morning was bad enough . . . but for the rest of the year?

"Teegan, Carter?" Mr. Hoffstedder called. I perked up. I hadn't seen Carter when I came in, but he was in the back of the room, on the opposite side from the door. His sun-streaked hair always smelled of coconut shampoo, and his green eyes scrambled my insides.

I'd had a crush on Carter since we started HoHo: He was cute, quiet, and fit in. There was nothing outstanding about him except for those green eyes—even his personality was kind of muted: not a class clown, not a jock, just . . . a guy. But even though we had classes together he acted like he never saw me. For a moment, I wondered if the "oink" note in homeroom *wasn't* meant to be mean. Maybe Carter sent it as a way to get my attention? We could laugh at how doll-like Dezzie looked sitting in the big desk, or maybe he'd help me escort her all over the building. . . . Too bad he wasn't *in* my homeroom. I wondered what he'd done over the summer, and if maybe this was the year I'd finally get up the nerve to talk to him. And too bad that with Dezzie on the scene, there was no way I'd even try. Hello, embarrassing!

"Yo, Hamlet," Ely said, nudging me and breaking my concentration. I dragged my gaze away from Carter.

"Huh?" I'd forgotten what we were saying.

"Seriously. She's here?" he said. Ely spent every summer with his grandmother on Block Island, and hadn't been home when my fate was sealed. And he hadn't believed it when Ty and I both IM'ed him about it. Like I could ever come up with something so horrifying as a joke. Mr. Hoffstedder began discussing expectations for the term.

"Seriously."

"Girl genius is rockin' the HoHo art wing this year to ruin Ham's life," Ty summarized for me. Really, it was all that needed to be said.

"Ms. Kennedy," the voice from the front of the room redirected my attention. "I think you'll be particularly interested in our inter-disciplinary project this term." Mr. Hoffstedder was giving me a wide smile that made my heart stop. There was only one reason why a teacher would single me out—

"We'll be doing an eight-week co-taught segment on Elizabethan England and Shakespeare with Mrs. Wimple. If you look at your schedules, English and history are blocked this year, so you'll be in class with the same students for both. This will allow Mrs. Wimple and me to give complementary assignments . . ."

I stopped listening, trying to get my heart beating again. The only thing worse than having Dezzie follow me around eighth grade was spending the term studying the Bard, as my parents called him. Shakespeare is for high school and college students—not eighth-grade public school English and social studies! I dropped my head to my desk.

I'd worked really hard during sixth and seventh grade to be average on the social scene—not noticable, not dorky enough to be worth teasing. HoHo was my refuge from my parents, their over-the-top Elizabethan home life, and my sister's smartness. All I wanted to do was keep flying under the radar, but Dezzie—and now this Shakespeare assignment—would put me in everyone's crosshairs

"At least you'll get A's in this stuff," Ely whispered, trying to make me feel better.

That was the problem. If I got A's in Shakespeare, I'd stick out at school. If I got B's in Shakespeare, I'd stick out at home.

For the first time, my parents would not only know about what I was doing in school, they'd *care*. Like, scarily much. Like, maybe as much as they cared about the work that Dezzie did. Getting really into a hobby just wasn't my thing.

I'd tried to find something I was good at, or cared about as much as the stuff my parents and sister loved:

I tried softball, but was too afraid to swing the bat. Especially after I hit the catcher with it.

Ballet was out—picture a duck on land. *And* I hated standing on my toes.

And let's just say that the mother/daughter Weaving & Dyeing camp my mom brought me to after fifth grade in an effort to "develop joint interests" wasn't a good fit. Mom made a nice sweater, though.

I was over trying new things—or "searching for my passion," as my dad put it. Done. There wasn't anything special about me—no gift, no talent, no super-smarts. Once I realized that, I embraced my averageness with relief. It meant no nutty Kennedy-family obsession, no bizarre activities, and my family left me alone.

Until now.

ᴄ·iV·ᴠ

The Scene: *The dinner table. Could be any night of the week. Mom, Dad, Dezzie, and Hamlet sit around a giant tray of steaks and baked potatoes.*

Dad: But they still do not know who killed Christopher Marlowe.

Dezzie (slicing her meat): It happened either in a bar or tavern. There is a rumor that he was a spy for Sir Francis Walsingham's intelligence service. But I am not sure he was really murdered.

Mom (knife clatters to her plate): You are not suggesting what I think you are!

Me (pouring gravy into mashed potato volcano): . . .

Dad: Marlowe DID NOT fake his death and write under the Shakespeare pseudonym. You have been reading too much Calvin Hoffman.

Dezzie: But the theories he puts forth are invigorating!

Me (watching gravy flow down the sides of
   the volcano): . . .

And it goes on and on: Me, with about as much to offer as
an empty plate, and them—and her—eating one another up.

Lost in my nightmares, I didn't hear a word Mr. Hoffstedder said during the rest of class. When the bell rang,
Ty turned around in his seat, his face set and serious. "It's
beginning, isn't it?"

"What?" I stuffed my textbook and papers in my book
bag.

"The Reign of Desdemona." He was trying to be funny,
but the truth really wasn't.

"Pretty much," I replied. I zippered the pocket closed.
"Speaking of her, I need to get downstairs and bring her
to our next class. See you in English?" He and Ely waved
good-bye and I made my second building-length sprint
of the day.

Dezzie was alone in the music hall when I arrived.

"How'd it go?" I asked, pointing her in the direction of
Stairwell A and the art room.

She shrugged. "Satisfactorily. She played several different types of music on the piano and explained identifying
elements of each. It will be an easy class for me. Oh, and
I met some girls. We had to work in a group and I was
paired with them."

We'd reached the door.

"Who were they?" I asked.

We entered the room just as the late bell rang. Of course. At first, every seat appeared full. Then I spotted waving arms at a tall table in the far corner.

"Hey! Over here!"

The arm-wavers were Saber Greene and Mauri Lee—witnesses to my morning humiliation, queens of annoyance, and the girls I tried to avoid at all cost.

"Them," Dezzie said, grabbing my hand and pulling me toward their table.

I was too shocked to yank my hand from hers. Dezzie'd spent one class period at HoHo and my life was already shuffled like a deck of cards. I'd spent nearly two years staying far away from Saber and Mauri, and now would sit face-to-face with them for the whole term.

When we were in sixth grade, Saber had seen me with my parents working at the county Renaissance Faire. In Ye Olde Costume Boothe. Going to a Renaissance Faire itself isn't necessarily embarrassing, but working at one, outfitted in the standard "Children's Tunic and Head-covering," is. Especially when you're eleven, and your father, who is wearing tights, drags someone you just met in junior high into the "Merry Maypole" dance. And makes her wear a "proper biggin"—a glorified handker-chief pinned to her head—because she'd ignored the "no bare heads" rule of the Faire. And several of your new classmates happen to be there for someone's birthday party and witness the whole thing. Saber and I hadn't spoken since . . . unless you count her repeated renditions of "Hamlet's Daddy Dresses Like a Lady" at lunch that year.

Now I was the one getting dragged across the room to something I didn't want to do. Dezzie finally dropped my hand. We stowed our bags on the shelf under the table and perched on the stools, Dezzie climbing up on hers. My heart pounded and I gave Saber and Mauri a smile so tight I was sure my face would crack with the effort. They returned it with wide, sickly sweet grins. Wolf grins. At the front of the room, a young teacher with hair the color of an almost-ripe tomato stood up.

"Welcome back. I'm Ms. Finch-Bean, and I'll be teaching art this year."

"What happened to Mrs. Higgins?" someone—it sounded like Mark Sloughman—called. Mrs. Higgins was old and let us do just about anything we wanted, as long as it involved construction paper and washable markers. Art was a blow-off class.

"She broke her hip over the summer. She might be back in January, but maybe not."

"Why didn't you tell us that you had such a cute little sister, Hamlet?" Saber asked, her voice low. Clearly, she'd had enough of Ms. Finch-Bean's introduction. She twirled the end of her French braid around one finger.

"She's adorable," Mauri said. She gave a toothy smile—all the better to eat me with. Both Saber and Mauri were wearing miniskirts and tees, and the minis made it hard for them to sit on the round art stools. They kept fidgeting and tugging at their hems. Dezzie also noticed.

"Wearing a longer dress or skirt would allow you to be more comfortable," she pointed out.

"Like you?" Mauri asked. Her voice sounded innocent, but it was a sneer in disguise. Dezzie glanced down at her trapeze shirt and leggings, which was a cute outfit for a seven-year-old. Unfortunately for Dezzie, the "dignified" clothes that she wanted weren't available in kids' sizes. I counted my blessings that she hadn't chosen to wear breeches, or the replica Chinese Red Army uniform that she designed when she was working on her Communism immersion project. You just never knew with her.

But right after that thought came a flash of annoyance. As weird as Dezzie was, and as hard as this day had been so far, I didn't want anyone to make fun of her, least of all these two. I opened my mouth to tell Mauri where to go, but Dezzie beat me to it.

"Well, I see that fashion wears out more apparel than the man," Dezzie added, a twinge of sarcasm in her voice. One of Mom's favorite Shakespeare quotes.

Saber and Mauri glanced at each other, clearly confused. I fought against a giggle.

"Whatever," Saber finally muttered. She tugged at the hem of her skirt again.

Even though I told Dezzie not to use any Shakespeare, their reaction was worth it.

Her limit for pre-class chatting reached, Dezzie turned her back to them and faced the front of the room. Her posture reminded me of the way she sat in homeroom, which made me think of that note again. Who'd written it? Why was it bugging me so much?

"So, Ham-let," Mauri said, chopping the syllables of my name, "why haven't we met Des-de-mo-na before?"

I wasn't sure how to answer that, or what Dezzie had told them in music appreciation. The glances and smiles they exchanged grated on my nerves.

"Ladies," Ms. Finch-Bean said, saving me from responding, "I need your attention up here, please." The three of us, copying Dezzie, sat straighter and faced forward.

Ms. Finch-Bean explained that we would be starting the year studying twentieth-century art movements and styles—abstract expressionism, surrealism, and pop art. Although the terms didn't mean anything to me, I recognized some of them from book titles Dezzie had taken out of the library for a mini immersion project on life after World War II. Ms. Finch-Bean passed around some pictures of paintings that didn't look like anything—just big splatters of red, black, white, and gray paint on a white canvas. Weird.

"These are in a museum somewhere?" said Saber. Her tone said she didn't believe it.

"Jackson Pollock painted them," Dezzie replied. "They're pure emotion." I could see what she meant—the painting looked angry in the middle, with all the colors together, but the splatters on the edges looked less mad. I thought of how when I get upset, it starts with a bunch of little things, then it all builds and builds to a big tangle of messy experiences. Like having Dezzie go to school with me. Or trying to be normal in a family of Bard Brains.

"They're a pure *mess*," Mauri said, and flipped her hair. "I think they're dumb."

"Really?" said Dezzie.

"Me too," echoed Saber. Dezzie turned to me. I shrugged and was about to respond, when Ms. Finch-Bean cut me off by asking that we pass the photos forward.

"They are dumb only to the uninitiated," Dezzie muttered, gray eyes as dark as rain clouds. I didn't have time to relish in the shocked expressions on Saber's and Mauri's faces, however, because class was over and I had to bring Dezzie back to the music hall so I could sprint to English.

V

Mrs. Wimple announced the same interdisciplinary Shakespeare extravaganza as Mr. Hoffstedder had in history. I guess my sigh was a little too loud, because it received a quizzical look from her, and a whispered "Did you think he was *lying?*" from Ty.

"We'll be reading *A Midsummer Night's Dream* and discussing elements of the play as they relate to your history class," Mrs. Wimple explained. A row of paperbacks waited for us on her bookshelf. "Mr. Hoffstedder and I will also be giving complementary assignments . . ." I tuned her out, stewing in Shakespeare's shadow.

As a distraction, I reached into my pocket and ran my hands around the edge of the note. *Had* Carter written it, and given it to someone else to send to my homeroom? It was a possibility, but an unlikely one. Even so, I let myself imagine he *had* written it, and that after class he'd wait for me in the hall to ask if I'd traveled this summer, or what movies I'd seen. I'd smile and answer—lying because I didn't think he'd be interested in the Shakespeare festival we went to in July—and then he'd offer to walk me to my next class—

And, thanks to Girl Genius, I'd have to say no.

After English, slightly annoyed that she'd prevented my imagination from enjoying a daydream, I raced to the music hall to get Dezzie, dropped her off at The Learning Center, then went back up to Mr. Symphony's room for pre-algebra. I was irritated, frazzled, and exhausted, and the day wasn't even half over.

I didn't even have the chance to say hi to my friend Judith, whom I'd blown by in the hall, and barely beat the tardy bell. Judith and I met sixth grade, when we had lockers next to each other. She goes to music camp all summer, and I'd been looking forward to catching up with her.

However, I *was* in time to see Mr. S. get all excited explaining how letters substitute for numbers in algebra. Right away I knew I'd need Dezzie's help for this class. From the expression on Ely's face, he would too. It was one of the best and worst parts of having an encyclopedia for a sister—I'd had a built-in homework helper since she was five, but seeing her hunched over a textbook, explaining history or math or science to Ty or Ely made me feel lame and awkward, and not at all like the older sister.

When math was over, I met Dezzie at TLC and brought her to the front office so Mom could pick her up. She must have thought Dezzie wouldn't come back in one piece, because the expression on her face when we came around the corner was one of pure relief.

"How were your classes?" Mom asked, swooping in like a vampire in a velvet cloak. The tassels fluttered at my sister's nose. She grimaced. I rolled my eyes. "Did you like them? Were you challenged enough?" Mom wasn't giving her time to breathe, let alone answer. None of the questions were aimed in my direction. Sometimes, being with my parents and Dezzie was like being the ground underneath a rainbow and a pot of gold: They went together perfectly, while I was just part of the scenery.

I coughed, attempting to get her attention. They both glanced my way, Mom's bun coming loose and tendrils waving around her head, Medusa-like.

"I'm going to go to lunch now, okay?"

Mom scowled.

"I *am* going to go to lunch now. Is that all right?" I tried again.

This time, Mom nodded. "Thank you, Hamlet, for taking care of Desdemona this morning," she said. "Your father and I greatly appreciate it."

Dezzie gave me a big smile.

That was a surprise. Usually, Dezzie duty was an obligation—something I had to do because she was my younger sister—so thanks were rare. Of course, Dezzie didn't need much minding—just walking her to the library or staying home if Mom and Dad were out and she had to meet her tutors. She didn't get into the same trouble as most seven-year-olds. Okay, she didn't get into trouble. Period. Which made any little trouble I got into look really big by comparison.

"You are welcome," I said, wearing the thanks like a too-small jacket. "See you this afternoon." I turned and headed toward the caf. The buzz of Mom's insistent questions trailed me down the hall.

For the first time, I had the chance to stop at my locker and stash my books. It felt like I was lugging rocks up and down the stairs all morning. When I put them in and grabbed my lunch, I was lighter. By about fifty short, smart, curly-haired pounds.

Just before I closed the door, however, I caught sight of something stuck in one of the vents. I tugged, and a folded piece of paper slid out and into my palm: an origami pig.

Was this from the note-writer? I turned it over, inspecting it for any marks. There was nothing on it—just plain notebook paper—but even holding it in my hand gave me a funny electric feeling. Was someone messing with me? Was this because of Dezzie? I had no idea.

I put Piglet back in my locker and closed the door, trying to close off the questions floating around my brain. There were too many other things to think about today; I'd get back to Piggy later.

Once inside the caf, I looked for Ty, Judith, and Ely at our usual table, but there were a bunch of seventh graders sitting there. The room was packed—was it more crowded than last year?—and everywhere I turned, it seemed, there were kids I didn't recognize. Great.

Spotting sixth graders was easy: They clustered at their tables like they were afraid of attack, or wore identical expressions of joy at finally finding elementary school friends. I stood, marooned in the center of the caf, searching for a familiar face, almost wishing I were back in sixth grade—at least my feelings would match the situation.

"Hey, Ham!" I caught my name above the rumble of conversation and clatter of trays. Turning, I scanned the room for the yeller.

"Over here!" An arm waved from the eighth-grade table area. Of course! I'd been so busy worrying about Dezzie, I'd forgotten that my lunch table would have relocated. With a mixture of pride (at being able to sit in the best section of the caf) and embarrassment (that I hadn't remembered earlier), I headed over to the waver.

Um, yeah.

I should have been paying better attention.

"I didn't even see you guys," I began, plopping my lunch bag onto the table and pulling out a chair. "I can't believe I forgot that—" I froze. Instead of Ty, Ely, Judith, and the others in our lunch bunch, my brown bag was parked next to Saber Greene, Mauri Lee, Carter Teegan, and his buddies KC Rails and Mark Sloughman. "I forgot that . . . uhhh . . ." I was stuck half in and half out of my seat, unsure of where to go. At the sight of Carter, my heart pounded and cheeks flushed. So *not* the smooth reaction that I'd imagined when we finally had lunch together.

"Sorry," I gulped, deciding to stand. "I thought I saw someone—"

"Waving?" Saber finished. I nodded, hoping my face didn't show my internal misery. If I hadn't had to drag Dezzie all over school, I'd be with my own friends, at our new table, not suffering my zillionth awkward situation of the day. Sneaking a glance at Carter, I saw that he was paying more attention to opening his bag of chips than me. KC, on the other hand, was staring straight at me. His reddish brown hair stood up like a spiky crown. He crossed his eyes. I'd seen him more so far today than I had in the previous two years combined, when he'd spent almost as much time in detention as in class.

"That was me," said Mauri, redirecting my attention. She had a small tray of what looked like sushi spread in front of her. When we visited my aunt Hope in New York last year before the annual Shakespeare convention, she took me out to try it. Due to the seventeenth-century cookbook Mom's been working on for the past year, I'm used to eating large chunks of beef and pork, so it was a good change. But, really, who brings sushi for lunch in junior high?

Then Mauri's words sunk in.

"You?"

"Mm-hmm," she said. She plucked a seaweed-wrapped roll off her tray and popped it into her mouth. Pieces of rice got stuck under her purple-polished nails, so she sucked them out. Icky! So icky!

"Oh."

"You can sit, you know," Saber said, sounding like their pack leader.

"Hey, Spamlet," KC said. I ignored him. KC was one of those guys who was always geeking out, doing something weird, something that made him the center of attention.

"So," Saber continued, "tell us about your sister. She looks a little young to be a sixth grader, and she's in our art and music classes. Where is she?" She twirled the end of her braid. A container of yogurt and an untouched peach sat in front of her.

Dezzie hadn't done much explaining.

"She's just here in the morning," I said, stammering over my words. They came in clusters, like grapes. Immediately, I hated myself for sounding so lame. Then I hated their lame questions.

"Eat," Mauri said, gesturing to my bag.

Obediently, I unpacked my lunch—an apple, a small package of cookies, turkey on wheat . . . and the Shakespeare Quote of the Day, firmly taped to my sandwich bag. I'd *told* my dad not to do that this year.

"To sleep, perchance to dream," KC read it aloud before I could stuff it back into the bag. The Wolf Queens snickered.

"Wish I could dream instead of being here all day," Carter muttered.

"I know *who* I'd dream about," KC said, nudging him. Then he winked at me.

Ew! I wished this *were* a dream. Where was Ty? But I was afraid that if I took my eyes off the table to search for him, I'd end up as lunch for this group.

"So . . . your sister," Saber continued. "Where is she? What's up with her in the afternoons?"

Why was she so interested? My sandwich bread was dry in my throat. I swallowed hard before answering, taking time to choose my words. "She takes other classes in the afternoon."

KC and Mark were staring straight at me. Carter was working his way through the bag of chips, munching loudly.

"Where does she go?" Saber prodded.

The warning bell buzzed, signaling five minutes to the end of the period. I balled up my bag, sandwich barely touched, apple heavy at the bottom, probably smashing my cookies.

"Gotta go," I said, springing from the chair like a jack-in-the-box. From the corner of my eye, I'd spotted a hurt-looking Ty slinking toward the door. I bolted from the table to catch up, but lost him in the crush of kids.

* * *

The good thing: In the afternoon I didn't have to run all over the building, so that sizzly fried-egg feeling started to go away.

Ty and I had agreed to meet at the flagpole and go home together, and part of me was afraid he wouldn't be there when I showed up. The quad was nearly empty by the time I arrived, and I spotted him right away: baggy jeans, green T-shirt, sitting on a wall fiddling with a wheel on his skateboard. He hated leaving it locked in the front office all day. It was his love.

"Hey," I said, wanting to sound normal.

"Hey." He didn't look up.

My stomach dipped.

"I wanted to find you at lunch today," I tried.

He spun a wheel.

I waited.

The wheel buzzed its circle. He finally peeked up at me from under his bangs.

"You found people to sit with pretty quick," he said. I cringed. His Saber issue had started in the fourth grade, when she'd showed a note he wrote to her asking if she knew if Mauri liked him to all the girls in our class.

"It's not like that," I said. I explained what had happened in art, and how they quizzed me about Dezzie. As I spoke, Ty nodded and watched me, laying his skateboard to one side. My stomach evened out. We were okay.

"So," I finished, "I think that's why they waved me over at lunch. I just assumed it was you." We were walking now, passing out of the school gates and heading home. Finally.

Ty was quiet. His thinking face was on—mouth turned down at the corners, eyes squinty. "Why do you think they're so interested in your sister?" he asked after a minute or so.

"I have no idea. Because she's new? And little?"

"Maybe," Ty agreed. "But there's gotta be more reasons why. Saber and Mauri aren't just nice to people because they're new. And you're not new."

I didn't know how to answer Ty's question. There was no reason for Saber and Mauri to be interested in me *or* Dezzie. They were a pair—a snarky, sparkly matched set. And they had no use for average people who'd dull their shine.

I was about to mention that to Ty, but then it hit me: Dezzie, of course, was anything *but* average.

Yikes.

ᑯ Vi ᴺ

That night after dinner, as I crossed the kitchen on my way upstairs to finish some annoying first-day homework, I heard, "Now, Desdemona, let's try it again," from the den. I crept closer to the door, wanting to keep out of sight. Something in my dad's tone was different from the usual "lecture voice" that he used when working with my sister.

"Hi, new student. That's a nice book bag you have there."

Dezzie's tiny voice responded, "Thank you."

"Would you like to buy some drugs? They will make you smarter."

WHAT?! I crammed both hands over my mouth and doubled over, trapping the giggles that wanted to escape. Dad must have *really* felt that the kids at HoHo were out to get Dezzie.

"No, thank you. Drugs are bad." Dezzie's voice sounded like it was coming from a doll—dry, flat, and emotionless. "Do we have to continue with this, Father?" she asked. "It is utterly ridiculous. I highly doubt that anyone at Howard

Hoffer Junior High School will offer me illicit substances or, if they do, that it will be done in such a straightforward, unambiguous way. Did you do this with Hamlet when she matriculated there?"

Nope, they hadn't. They'd given me a short lecture as a sixth grader about "being my own self" and watching the crowd I associated with, and that was it. I wasn't laughing anymore. What would Dad say?

"Your sister was substantially older than you when she entered junior high school. You are vulnerable in a different way than she." So I hadn't gotten the drugs talk because I was older and less vulnerable? That's it?

A little annoyed with that answer—how about, "We trust her and she didn't need a lecture," instead?—I decided that Dezzie needed rescuing. I went back into the kitchen and rummaged around loudly for a glass of water. Dad and Dezzie emerged from the den, followed by Iago, our white puffball of a dog. A colleague of my parents' who took a new job in Norway gave him to us. Dad was wearing his bee T-shirt: There were two bees on the back, the word "or," and, below that, two bees with that red circle with the slash through it over them. Get it?

Yeah.

He thinks it's hysterical.

"I need to find my lecture notes for Birth of the Sonnet. Desdemona and I were discussing the skills she will need to navigate the junior high school."

"Oh," I said. What other "skills" did he think Dezzie might need? Archery? Because that would be as useful at HoHo as his other pointers. My parents spent too much time in their school offices. They needed to get out more. Lots more.

"Hamlet said she'd help me earlier today," Dezzie said.

Had I? Then I remembered our conversation in the stairwell.

Dad seemed both hopeful and relieved. "Can you talk to her about the self-possession needed to attend junior high school? Your mother comes home at nine." He said the last part with a tone that meant: "I'm supposed to be doing this and she will kill me if she sees you doing so. Be finished by then."

I shrugged. "No problem." (Unlike Mom and her contractions, Dad lets us get away with using slang occasionally).

Dad disappeared in the direction of his office, and Iago lay down on his purple pillow in the corner of the kitchen.

"So how'd it go with your socialization lessons?" I asked. I giggled at the memory.

Dezzie rolled her eyes. "You heard that? I know that our parents share a heavy burden of anxiety regarding my well-being at Howard Hoffer, but truly, Hamlet, you would think that I didn't know any better . . . that I was . . ." She searched for the word.

"Average?" I offered.

"Precisely," she replied.

"Okay," I told her. "But if you really want to survive HoHo, you need to know how to act normal."

"But I am not what one would consider 'normal,' due to my age and intellect," Dezzie pointed out. "It would be contradictory for me to act in the way of a standard student."

"True," I said, frustrated. For a smart kid, you'd think my sister would be able to understand everyday life better. "But junior high is not about standing out. It's about fitting in."

"Why?"

A bunch of answers came to mind: a.) Because that's how it *is.* b.) Because no one wants to stand out. c.) Because it's easier that way.

"I don't know." Even my average brain knew none of those responses were good ones.

"Although I cannot fully comprehend the necessity of compromising myself for the sake of assimilating to the group, I trust your experience in the matter.

"I am ready for my lessons," she said. "Teach away."

We moved upstairs into my bedroom, where, for the next hour and a half, I taught Dezzie everything I could possibly think of regarding the social rules and regulations of HoHo Junior High. Some of the highlights:

* Unlike at home, slang, "commoner's speech," and contractions are a communication necessity
* "Huzzah!" and other Elizabethan terms are not effective communication tools
* Blending in is the ultimate goal
* Smart kids do not blend in. Answering too many questions in class, raising your hand too often, and being too friendly with the teachers will classify you as a "nerd" or "geek," which is highly undesirable.

I mentioned that one specifically because Dezzie would "blend in" around HoHo about as easily as a squash blends in with motorcycles—without answering every question that she heard walking through the halls.

As I listed the rules, her eyes sparkled. She was getting her "intellectually engaged" look: furrowed brow, lips in a smirk, eyebrow cocked—an expression that I'd seen more often on teachers and my parents and their friends than anyone under the age of forty . . . except Dezzie.

"What are the consequences to behaving outside of the norm?" she asked.

I tried to find an answer that was better than the "I don't know" I'd given her earlier. "People might tease you, or you might not have someone to sit with at lunch or during activities. Sometimes, depending on what you do, people can be mean," I tried. Hearing it out loud made

44

it sound a lot lamer than it was in real life, and it did nothing to capture the feeling of being ignored, or the coldness that could creep around your heart when you realized that you were being shut out.

"It's the preadolescent sociological phenomenon at work, isn't it? Queen bees on the playground?" she asked. "Fascinating. I've read about it, of course, but to experience it firsthand will be a treat."

I had no idea what she was talking about, but she was probably right . . . although I'm not sure I would classify experiencing junior high as "a treat." But her excitement helped me feel a little less guilty about what I was doing: asking her to hide everything that made Dezzie, Dezzie.

Then we got practical: open classroom seating situations, how to carry a backpack without looking like a dork (*never* clip the waist belt), and never mentioning "immersion projects" or outside HoHo academics.

Through it all, Dezzie took notes and nodded in the right places. Just before nine, I suggested that we wrap it up. Mom would be home soon, and I didn't want to have to answer any uncomfortable questions. Dezzie nodded, but her brow was knitted as tightly as one of Mom's loom sweaters.

"Do you think I can do it, Ham?" she asked, gray eyes searching mine. "There are a lot of things to remember."

A funny pulling sensation happened around my heart. I pushed it away. I was doing what was best for her, wasn't I?

"Of course I do. You're the best student ever." I gave her a big fake smile.

Her eyebrows relaxed. "Not ever, but close to it," she said. "This is a different kind of learning, though." She shrugged. "I've gotta take my bath . . . How did that sound?"

For a minute, I didn't understand what she meant. Then I got it.

"Rockin'," I said, then grinned.

She tucked her notes under one arm and slipped out of my room, clicking the door closed. I flopped back on my bed, hoping it would work, hoping Dezzie would become part of the HoHo fabric, hoping that eighth grade would be okay.

I turned my computer on. The IM tone blinged right away.

> tyboardr11: Wee genius back @ HoHo 2morrow?
> greeneggs22: yup.
> tyboardr11: u?
> greeneggs22: have 2.
> tyboardr11: if she wreks ur life u cld always join the Ren Faire circus

Pretty much.

> greeneggs22: Huzzah!

ᐤ Vii ᐤ

That first week, my parents wanted daily updates of the classes at HoHo. I let Dezzie do all the talking at the dinner table. *Big* mistake.

"In art, we are making abstract expressionist paintings, like Jackson Pollock's. Saber and Mauri, with whom we sit, do not like them very much, but they are looking forward to the Salute to Shakespeare project in English and history."

I could have fallen off my chair. I hadn't told my parents anything about our exploration of the Bard.

"Do tell!" My mother put down her fork and pushed back the sleeves of her nubby hand-loomed sweater. It was Sunday, which was seventeenth-century chicken stew night . . . which was *way* better than "potage of mutton" night. Honestly, I wasn't sure what a "potage" was, even though I had to eat it.

"What is this about?" my father said, giving us his full attention. He'd been skimming student sonnets while we ate.

I glared at Dezzie.

"Do not give your sister a cross look," Dad admonished. When I sat back in my chair, he continued. "Now, explain to us about this Shakespeare event going on at school."

"Dezzie can tell you," I said, and folded my arms. Her eyes went big. She could tell I wasn't happy, but I bet it didn't occur to her as to why. Sharing her "intellectual pursuits" with my parents came as naturally to her as calculus or four-syllable words. Iago, who'd been sleeping under the table, hopped into her lap.

"Well," she began, "some of the English and history classes are studying Shakespeare and Elizabethan England." She patted Iago's head, speaking to him more than us.

My mother brought her hands to her chest in two excited fists. "Marvelous! What a wonderful opportunity for the students!" At home, when she's not dressed in her regalia, Mom wears pleated broomstick skirts with those handmade sweaters and "stocks and socks"—Birkenstock sandals with big, thick woolen socks. Sometimes I don't know which is more mortifying—being out in public with her in a costume, or the thought of someone showing up unexpectedly and seeing her "loungewear."

"Agreed," said Dad. I pretended that I didn't exist, praying to the ghosts of geeks past they would be so excited at the *thought* of junior high kids learning about Shakespeare that they wouldn't actually ask the question that made the most sense. It had happened before.

"Is your English class one of the ones studying the Bard, Hamlet?" Mom asked. She gave me her professor stare: narrow eyes, tight lips.

So much for my prayers.

For a moment, I considered lying. If I said no, there was a chance that they'd forget about it, or at least only question Dezzie about the class. But they'd find out eventually. Best to get it over with now.

"Yes," I replied. Shock flitted across Mom's face, Dad's showed mild curiosity.

"Why did you not tell us?"

"Because I wanted to surprise you," I explained. And because it's only been the first week of school, I added in my head. And I don't want any more Shakespeare-o-rama in my life. "I thought it would be more fun that way."

Their faces changed to mirrors of happiness and pride.

"Perhaps we will make ourselves available to consult," Dad said.

"Consult?" I coughed the word out. "Like, help?"

"Why, yes," Mom added. "It would be a lovely way to be involved in your studies."

No it wouldn't.

"Uh, well, let me check with my teacher," I said lamely. Shock spread through my body. "I will let you know what she says."

Dezzie, probably figuring out what had gone wrong, changed the subject to a calculus problem and the conversation moved away from me. Although relieved, I now had to figure out how to avoid any parental involvement in "Salute to Shakespeare." And that would be about as easy as identifying the ingredients in potage of mutton.

In my room later, Dezzie apologized.

"I am sorry I told, Hamlet," Dezzie said. She was wearing her *Finding Nemo* pajamas—the ones with fish on the pants and a picture of the turtles on the top—and her long hair was still damp from her bath.

And I could tell that she truly was. Not that it made me feel any better. I kept her age secret at school; the least she could have done was keep my coursework off Mom and Dad's radar screen. I stretched out across my bed and knocked my math book onto the floor with my foot.

"Are you mad at me?" She stood in the doorway, leaning against the frame, big-eyed and quiet-voiced.

It's hard to be mad at someone who is barely four feet tall and wearing Nemo pants.

"No, Dez, I'm not mad at you," I said, feeling like a jerk for being upset.

She straightened and eyed me like a TV cop evaluating a criminal. "It's all right if you are. From now on, I will try and do my best not to share excess information."

Having a brainiac little sister is tough enough, but

when she's not only smart, but you kind of like her, that makes it even worse.

"It's fine," I said, taking a deep breath and finding some genuine forgiveness. I sat up, and she joined me on the bed, sitting cross-legged across from me.

Dezzie sighed. "I know I need the social development and the art credit," she said, changing the subject. "I just don't think Howard Hoffer is the best environment for me. I wish Mom and Dad would let me just do art and music at SMARTS over the summer."

SMARTS is the camp for gifted kids that Dezzie goes to each year. It's a way for children with high IQs to spend time with other kids like them, so they won't feel alone in their genius. Most of the kids that go are between nine and thirteen, but there are a couple who are Dezzie's age. They take classes (of course), but there's also a lot of encouragement to do camp-type stuff: arts and crafts, swimming, Topographic Beach Exploration . . . you know, the usual.

For the past three years, we've attended SMARTS Family Day—when the "campers" present mini-lectures on their coursework and the moms and dads ooh and ahh. The first year we were there, my parents made me go to a class called Siblings of Gifted Scholars. We had a group leader—an older brother to one of the former campers, who is now in medical school at fifteen. The leader guy was twenty, and he would try to encourage us to talk about

51

our "feelings of jealousy, inadequacy, or rage" toward our brilliant sisters and brothers.

The Scene: *A classroom at SMARTS camp. Eight or ten kids of various ages sit at desks pushed into a circle and wear bored expressions.*

Group leader: I always wished that my parents paid more attention to me. Do you ever feel this way?

No one responds. Girl with pink hair nods.

Group leader: These thoughts are perfectly normal. You are special too, you know.

Pink-hair girl looks like she's about to speak. A guy, who'd been leaning back in his chair, clicks all four feet to the ground.

Chair guy: Are you a psych major in college or something? 'Cause you've got some major issues. The only thing that sucks about my brother being a whiz is this lame camp that my parents bring us to every year. The rest of the time they leave me alone.

Pink-hair girl watches the floor. Everyone else nods.

Girl in dark denim dress: Yeah, it's sweet. They're so busy worrying about Jules that I can do whatever I want.

Group leader (sweat beading on forehead): Aren't you looking for some attention?

Don't you want your parents to be involved
with *you?*

Pink-hair girl leans forward in her chair, as though
to talk.

Me (surprised that I'm speaking): No way. The
less involved, the better.

Pink-hair girl slumps in her seat.

First guy: Can we go now? 'Cause I don't think
any of us really need to be here.

Group leader (swallows a few times): Urm,
well, I suppose. Although it's best not to
let these issues go untreated.

He calls out the last part as the group files from the room.

Every so often I wonder what that girl wanted to talk
about. Some days, I think I know—that it's hard, that nothing is normal, that being constantly behind someone else
is tiring, especially if they are younger than you. And it
may have been nice to hear it out loud.

So until now, Mom and Dad had always been so busy
making sure Dezzie grew into her intelligence, I'd had
free rein. I didn't have to worry about them showing up
to events wearing their Elizabethan collars, or picking me
up from school in cloaks. Even if I did get a little lonely
sometimes.

Right now, lonely was looking better and better.

ᴄViii~

T he next week went basically the same as the
first: I ran all over the school in the morning, making sure Dezzie was on time for
her classes, but barely getting to my own. I suppose I
could have said something to my teachers about why
I was nearly late every day, but why bother? It'd only draw
more attention to the oddity that was my life.

I did have time to keep an eye out for more notes or
pigs, but none appeared. I hadn't said anything to Ty
about it, because he'd probably get all boy-ish and say it
didn't mean anything. And he'd definitely shoot down my
idea that it was Carter. Maybe I'd tell Judith. In the mean-
time, the first one lived in a small pocket of my backpack,
providing a little mystery to my day.

Carter was not a mystery, however: He continued to
look through me like I was a nonthreatening ghost. Who
else could it *be?*

In English, Mrs. Wimple explained our major project.
We were supposed to pick any scene from Act I of *A Midsummer Night's Dream,* then set it up in a replica of the

theater we'd be building for history class. That meant we had to figure out what the characters looked like, place them on the stage, and be able to explain what scene we chose and why. Everyone complained because we hadn't even started reading the play yet, but Mrs. Wimple said that we'd have plenty of time.

"We'll get started right now. This is the story of four people who get lost in a forest one night," she explained. "Two of the men are in love with the same woman, but thanks to a fairy with a sense of humor, both end up in love with the *other* girl. Oh, and there's a jackass in the story." When she said that everyone gasped, then giggled.

"Yes," she continued, "I said *jackass*. Someone gets turned into one. You'll see what I mean." She handed out copies of the play. From across the aisle, I heard KC mumble, "*Some* people I know would make great jackasses."

He must have seen me smile in agreement—even though I didn't know who he was talking about; I could make my own list—because he added, "And some should just mind their own business."

My cheeks burned. What was *that* about?

"We'll be reading aloud," Mrs. Wimple continued. I turned my attention to her so I wouldn't encourage KC to say anything else irritating. "So we can get a feel for Shakespeare's language and characters. Who would like to volunteer? I need six of you for this scene."

Everyone's eyes immediately dropped to their book

covers. Reading out loud can be pretty awful, and the Bard doesn't exactly make things easy on a contemporary reader—at least, that's what my parents say. I also kept my head down. With a name like mine, why be singled out?

"Uh-huh," she said. "I guess I'm going to have to recruit my cast. Let's see . . . Julie, you read Hippolyta. KC, you are now Theseus, ruler of Athens. Nirmal, please read Egeus." She chose two other boys to be Lysander and Demetrius, and then proclaimed, "Tyler, you will read Hermia."

Ty's ears turned red. "But Mrs. Wimple! That's a girl's part!"

"A lot of the female characters were played by men in Shakespeare's time," I consoled, forgetting that I'd be better off keeping my knowledge to myself. "It's no big deal."

"Said well by the girl with the guy's name," KC responded, voice too low for the teacher to hear.

I wanted to slug him. I settled for glaring in his direction.

"Hamlet is quite correct," Mrs. Wimple said. "It's good to see that you feel comfortable sharing your knowledge of Elizabethan history. So perhaps you would like to read Hermia's lines instead?" She gave a little flourish with her hand for emphasis.

I could feel everyone staring at me. If my face got any hotter it would melt everything in a four-seat radius.

"Uh, well . . ." I started. Reading Shakespeare in my house

was a sport left to the professionals. I'd attended enough plays and read-throughs to last a lifetime, and had been forced, on two occasions, to play the role of "a soldier" in a dinnertime scene execution of—yes—*Hamlet.* I felt fine sitting this one out. "Uh, I think Ty will do a great job." I hoped he'd forgive me for throwing him back under the bus.

"Then perhaps you'll read Hippolyta for us, instead of Julie."

"Well," I tried. I glanced at Ty for help, but he was staring at a spot on the blackboard. Payback. "I'd rather . . ."

"Good," she said, snipping the word like her lips were scissors. "Let's begin, then."

I flipped to the beginning of the play. Theseus was talking about a wedding.

KC was reading Theseus like he was acting on a soap opera. "Now, fair Hippolyta, our nuptial hour"—he waggled his eyebrows at me—"draws on apace . . ."

"Respectfully, please," Mrs. Wimple corrected.

"Long withering out a young man's revenue," KC finished. I noticed that when he wasn't overdoing it, his voice sounded kind of warm reading the lines. Like honey.

Ew! I snapped out of some sort of Shakespeare-spell. KC was more like pickles than honey—sharp and stand-outy. Now Carter, on the other hand . . . he was like frosting: good to look at and sweet. Just thinking about him listening to me read made the back of my neck feel warm. My turn. I took a breath.

"Four days will quickly steep themselves in night/ Four nights will quickly dream away the time: and then the moon—like a silver bow/New-bent in heaven—shall behold the night of our solemnities." Theseus was supposed to speak next. I waited for KC's line. He didn't come in.

I glanced up.

Everyone in the class, including Mrs. Wimple, was staring at me. If my life was *actually* a cartoon, instead of just feeling like one, their jaws would be on the floor. Even Ty was gawking.

"Uhhh," I mumbled, feeling sweat bead on the back of my neck. Had I missed a line?

My noise thawed Mrs. Wimple from her freeze. "Well, Ms. Kennedy. I *am* impressed. How have you hidden this talent from us?" Her eyebrows bunched tight over her nose. I couldn't tell if she was mad or complimenting me. I turned to Ty, hoping he could explain. I'd never had Mrs. Wimple as a teacher before—and I wasn't hiding anything from anyone. What was going on?

The bell rang, ending class and busting the exaggerated stares. Backpacks were stuffed and zippered, and everyone started to leave. I also packed up.

"Hamlet, I'd like to speak with you for a moment," Mrs. Wimple said from her desk. I turned to Ty, who was half out of his chair.

"What is *UP?*" I hissed.

"Your reading," he whispered back, looking over his shoulder to Mrs. Wimple.

"*So?*" What had I done?

"Hamlet," he said gently. Ty *never* called me Hamlet. "You read it *perfectly.*"

"So?" What was the big deal?

"Mr. Spencer," Mrs. Wimple said, smoothing the front of her denim jumper, "I believe you'll be late to your next class if you don't move along." Ty scooted out of the room, leaving me with an apologetic glance and mouthing the word "lunch." I nodded, and then brought my stuff up to Mrs. Wimple's desk.

She was just sitting there, waiting for me, eyes glittering behind her round glasses. I couldn't read her expression—her lips were pressed into a line, but her cheeks were bunched tight, as though she was trying not to smile. She folded her hands on top of her ragged copy of *Midsummer.*

"So, Ms. Kennedy, have you been studying the play outside of class? Or acting in it?"

I shook my head, still confused. "I'm not sure what you mean," I pleaded. "Honest. Ty said something about the way I read, but I didn't do anything special. Just looked at the lines." My hands were sweating. I still needed to get my sister and walk her to her next class.

Mrs. Wimple sighed. "It's all right if you like Shakespeare," she said. "You don't have to pretend that you don't. If you're practicing with your parents, I'd just like

59

to know the strategies you're using." She leaned against the back of her chair and dropped her hands to her lap.

"But I'm not!" Why wouldn't she believe me? Would Dezzie make it to TLC okay without me? "My parents read the play to me before, but that was almost three years ago. Today I just flipped through the scene and checked my lines while KC was reading." I picked up her copy of the play and turned the pages like I had in class. The late bell buzzed and I jumped.

"I'll give you a pass," she said. "This is my free period. Finish showing me what you did, but pick another scene."

The last thing I wanted to do was read more Shakespeare— my mouth was so dry that I was sure my tongue was made of sand, but the rest of me was sweating like I'd just been hit by a wave. I turned one more page, then scanned the words. It was the scene after Puck gives Bottom a donkey's head. Mrs. Wimple leaned over. I tilted the book toward her.

"Read Puck," she instructed.

I sighed and swallowed, trying to get rid of that gritty-mouth sensation.

"I'll follow you, I'll lead you about a round, through bog, through brush, through brake, through brier./Sometime a horse I'll be, sometime a hound, a hog, a headless bear, sometime a fire;/and neigh, and bark, and grunt, and roar, and burn, like horse, hound hog, bear, fire at every turn." Mrs. Wimple was watching me covetously, like I was a rare species of child first discovered in her classroom.

"See? I read it."

"You didn't read it, Hamlet," she said, smile finally splitting her face. "You performed it. Quite beautifully." The way she said that made my stomach feel like someone had filled it with slippery fish. "I don't understand," I said, hoping for another explanation—one that would make sense and get rid of the uncomfortable shaking in my gut. I'd spent my whole life avoiding the Bard, and this was like finding out we were related.

"You may have read the lines from the text," Mrs. Wimple said. "But your inflection, pronunciation, and emotional content brought the character to *life*." Her face broke open into another wide smile, which made that stomach of sea creatures splash into my feet. "Shall we try it again?"

"I know what I did," I snapped, anger busting through the fear. "I *read*. And I don't want to do it again." Suddenly, all I wanted was to be sitting in Mr. Symphony's class, fumbling through pre-algebra. I tried to control my voice. "May I have a pass, please?"

"You have a gift, Hamlet, that you are surely wasting. It might seem like a burden now, but it is something that you owe yourself to explore. When you are adult enough to discuss it, let me know."

"I'd like a pass," I stated more firmly, staring at a spot over her head. "I need to go."

Mrs. Wimple made a hissing tsk-noise at my borderline disrespect. But she pulled out her pass packet and scribbled a note to Mr. S. When she handed it to me, I spun on my heels and walked out as fast as I could.

The deserted halls echoed with the murmurs coming from the classrooms. I went straight for the girls' bathroom on the second floor, trying not to think about Shakespeare, reading, or anything else the whole way there. When I reached it, I slammed my body through the door and locked myself in a stall. Angry tears flowed down my cheeks. My hands shook. I tried taking deep breaths to get control of myself. It was just a fluke, I reasoned, the breathing helping me calm down. I blew my nose on some toilet paper and swiped at my eyes. There was nothing to be upset about. I was just familiar with the lines because my parents practically talked in sonnets. I wasn't *performing* anything. I just understood more of Shakespeare's language, so my reading sounded better than the other kids'. Way better, evidently. That's why she thought I was performing—because if that *wasn't* it, I had a real problem:

There was nothing talentless, or average, about a girl who could spout Shakespeare like a pro. I knew it, Mrs. Wimple knew it, and my parents would too.

And the crazy of Dezzie and my parents would be nothing but shadows next to the spotlight that this fiasco would beam on me.

⌐iX⌐

By the time I left the bathroom and skidded—late—into pre-algebra, I'd convinced myself that if I ignored the whole thing, other people, Mrs. Wimple included, would too. It wasn't the best strategy, but it stopped the tears. I'd have time to figure it out later, when I was in the privacy of my room and not in danger of being scouted out by a hall monitor.

That didn't last too long. At lunch, Judith—who wasn't in my class, but had heard the story—kept asking me questions about what happened in English. I brushed her off.

"No biggie," I explained, trying to keep my voice light. "I knew that section because my parents had been working on the book with me at night. You know how *they* are."

Ely and Judith bought it. Ty, I could tell, wasn't convinced. He knew that: a.) I *never* worked on Shakespeare stuff with my parents, and b.) I was as shocked as he was when it went down. But he didn't say anything. I owed him a cone at our next Chilly Spoon trip for that one.

As if all of that wasn't bad enough, Saber and Mauri came by our table at the end of the period to rub it in, just as Ely was leaving for his meeting with James, the school counselor. Ely had an appointment with him every other week since his sister got leukemia when we were in sixth grade. She went through a rough time, but was okay now. After she got better, Ely said he liked hanging out with James, so he kept going.

"Heard you gave quite a performance today, Puck-face," Mauri sneered. "Showing off what you learned at home?" Next to her, Saber curtsied.

"Too bad Shakespeare wasn't around to see it," she said. "I heard it was Bard-tastic." The two of them giggled their way out of the lunchroom. I clenched my hands into tight fists and pushed my chair back.

"I should just . . ."

"Dude, not worth it," Judith cautioned. She steered me in the opposite direction. We stopped at our lockers, side by side in the main hall. When I turned the combination, I felt that jolt of electricity before I even saw it: another origami pig, stuffed into the vent. This one was wearing a blue ink smiley face and made from plain white printer paper. Was someone doing it to be mean? If they were, why draw a smiley face on it?

"What's that?" Judith leaned over my shoulder. I showed her the pig, and explained about its cousin and the homeroom note on our walk to science.

"You *so* have an admirer," she squealed. "Who do you think it is?"

I still had no idea. And with the way this year had started off, I wasn't too sure I wanted to find out.

After the English incident, I tried even harder to avoid drawing attention to myself. I wanted nothing more than to fade into the background and let everyone forget about my "performance." But Saber and Mauri were determined to drag at least one Kennedy onto center stage.

The Scene: *Art class, the following day. Kids hunched over paintings, washing brushes, talking. At one table sit Desdemona, Saber, Mauri, and me.*

Saber (chewing the end of her paintbrush): So . . . Dezzie. How do you like HoHo?

Dezzie (not looking up from her work): I am finding it satisfactory.

Mauri: Is it better than your other school?

Me (louder than I want to sound): Dezzie, can you pass me the blue?

Saber: What grade did you skip, Dezzie?

Avoiding their questions only made them ask more. It was like a pastime for them; I had no idea why they cared so much. And since they couldn't get any information out of Dezzie, they tried me. Whenever I passed them in the hall or walked by their table at lunch, I'd get a "Hiii Hamlet," in unison, and some question about where Dezzie was. Nothing was said in an outright mean way, but it was a little too friendly sounding, if you get me. I ignored them as best I could, adding them to my ever-growing list of things to avoid: making eye contact with Mrs. Wimple in English, thinking about what happened when I read Shakespeare out loud, and talking to my parents and teachers about their involvement in the Salute.

A day later, in history class Mr. Hoffstedder announced our theater assignment. Until now, we'd been learning the basics about Elizabethan England—class structure and nobility, the fact that people were dirty and smelly back then—stuff Mom and Dad talked about ever since I could remember. Only in a more positive, "I heart the 1600s" kind of way. Kind of like Dad's new shirt, which featured "Shakespeare is my homeboy" spelled out in block letters under a picture of the Bard.

"Your co-assignment is to build an accurate replica of the Globe Theatre, where Shakespeare's plays were performed, with a partner. Then each of you will write a short essay about why the theater was designed in such a specific way. This will be the history component of the assignment, and a way to illustrate your creativity."

Ty kicked the leg of my desk with his foot.

"Partners?" he whispered.

I nodded. I knew what would come next.

"Do you have any extras?"

I rolled my eyes at him. Building Globes was one of my father's hobbies. We had four in our basement already. This would be number five. So much for creativity—for us, this would be more like an exercise in repetition.

"We're going to have special judges from outside the Howard Hoffer community evaluate your work," Mr. Hoffstedder said. "They'll award prizes in three categories: accuracy of design, uniqueness of materials, and creativity in scene-staging. So be sure to put forward your best effort."

There was no way I'd tell my parents about the contest. Knowing that someone was going to come to school and judge my theater on its Globe-ness meant they'd focus with microscopic accuracy on every detail.

A seventeenth-century microscope, but still.

At the Chilly Spoon that day, Ty and I settled into our favorite table. Me with a peppermint stick sundae and Ty with two scoops of fudge mania in a cup, doused with chocolate sprinkles. I knew what was coming.

"So what really happened in English?" he asked. He stuffed a heaping spoonful into his mouth. I shrugged.

"I don't know. Wimple made me read another passage for her after, and said I did the same thing—I *emoted* it, or something." If I focused on eating around the whipped cream, I wouldn't have to see Ty's expression.

"What do you think you did?" I heard a few sprinkles

rain from his cup and bounce on the Formica table.

"I thought I was reading," I confessed. "I said the words I saw in front of me."

"You weren't reading," he said. "At least, not like I've ever heard anyone read."

"Then what was I doing? Why does everyone keep saying that?" I was getting frustrated. I folded the napkin to burn off some energy.

"Maybe you have a talent," Ty offered. "You're an actor."

"But I've been in plays before," I said. "And I wasn't so special then."

"Being a Native American in the fourth-grade Thanksgiving play doesn't count," Ty pointed out. "You had no lines. Maybe you're a Shakespeare-acting genius."

"I think that's what Wimple was hinting at," I admitted. "She wanted me to keep doing it to prove she was right." What if I *was* some kind of acting genius, and just didn't know it?

"The whole on-stage thing freaks me out. I'm going to beg Wimple to let me do lights or something for the performance," Ty said. "But I think it'd be pretty cool to be an actor."

"Not if it was Shakespeare you were good at acting out." I sighed. "And don't remind me about the performance part. It freaks me out too." Would Mom and Dad stick me onstage at the Ren Faire? Make me take acting classes, like Dezzie takes special academics? Would I be forced to participate in some sort of family troupe?

Ty glanced at me out of the corner of one eye, his bangs hanging in front of his face. "You know, it's not the worst thing in the world," he said, and stuffed another giant spoonful into his mouth. A sprinkle dotted his chin. It sounded like each of his words were glass bubbles that he didn't want to break.

"What's not?" My voice was sharp and stony.

"Having something in common with your family."

That sentence lingered in the air between us. A cold sensation, then a rush of heat, filled my body. If I had something in common with Dezzie and my parents, it meant I was like them—another freaky Kennedy. What if that was the case, and I was just better at hiding it?

That was the thought that scared me more than anything else.

ᴄ X ᴖ

hat Saturday, Ty, Ely, and Judith came over to get started on our Globe project. Ty got there first, and Mom beat me to the door.

"Master Tyler! So nice to see you." Ty's shoulders pulled up toward his ears in an anticipatory cringe. When Mom knows people well, they don't get a curtsy. She gave him a peck on each cheek and squeezed his shoulders in a quasi-hug.

Ty was one of the few people I felt comfortable having around my family. He's known us since before Dezzie was born, when things were slightly more normal around here. I don't think he's ever gotten used to my mom's ways of saying hi, though.

"Mom, don't kiss Ty like that. He doesn't like it," I said for the zillionth time. And for the zillionth time, she looked surprised and stepped away. For a bunch of smart people, it took them a long time to learn basic stuff.

"What are you working on?" she asked.

He and I shot glances at each other.

"We're building a replica of the Globe," Ty admitted.

"How wonderful! I will notify Roger anon. You two may retreat to the basement." She shooed us in that direction, white sleeves bellowing like sails attached to her arms.

The upstairs of our house looks pretty much like everyone else's—family pictures on the walls (okay, some are in Elizabethan attire), comfy furniture to sit on—with the addition of lots of books and papers stacked on tables, chairs, and any other flat surface. The basement is another situation altogether.

We have two finished rooms downstairs, and they're the only places where Iago isn't allowed—much to his irritation. One is set up like a family room, with a big fireplace and cozy chairs. The other is my dad's office. Both are filled with Shakespeare-related stuff.

Mom's Shakespeare collection sits on two shelves in the family room. And I don't mean the books. She actually collects Shakespeare himself—dolls, figurines, busts, plates, key chains—anything that looks like him. There are poseable action figures, mugs, and even a cow and a rubber duck both wearing Shakespeare outfits that some students gave her. There are framed pictures on the walls called "The Death of Ophelia" and "The Death of Romeo and Juliet"—you know, happy art like that—and there's even a bunch of photos from Stratford-on-Avon and one of his plaques at Westminster Abbey that Mom shot on a research trip. On the couch are pillows with Shakespeare quotes embroidered on them (Gram, who tolerated Mom's nuttiness but didn't really get it, made them before she died), and in one corner we have a suit of armor.

Yes, a real one.

Dad bought it at an auction at a British castle and shipped it home in pieces. It weighs a ton, and they've never let me or Dezzie try it on, even though it'd be too small for anyone else to wear. Go figure—it's the only cool thing we own. I think they're afraid that we won't be able to get out.

Dad's office is a mess. There are books and papers everywhere, as well as fifteen years worth of lost lecture notes. The only thing that he keeps neat is his Globe Theatre collection. He started building them a couple of summers ago, and he makes them out of different materials. I asked him why he did it—they all look the same, after all—and he said it was because he enjoyed the feeling of re-creating something so special over and over again. Sometimes I wonder why not try designing something new that's special, but he likes doing it, so it's not really any of my business.

Ty and I cleared off space on the large coffee table. Before I was born, Dad built it as an anniversary gift for my mom. It's made of really heavy wood, and he put copies of Elizabethan England–era maps all over the top of it, then covered them with about eight inches of varnish, so nothing can stain them and the table will never get wrecked. It looks kind of cool, actually.

Hoping to be spared several dinnertime lectures of information and "helpful hints," I hadn't told my dad about the Globe project in advance, so Ty had downloaded Build a Globe Theatre plans from the Internet. We spent the first few minutes trying to figure out how to follow the directions.

Ty laid a basic foundation, and then the basement door opened. Dad came downstairs, wearing the big goofy grin that he only gets when we pull into the Ren Faire parking lot. And his "Shakespeare hates your emo poems" T-shirt. It's his favorite.

"I heard that someone down here is doing some pretty exciting work," he said.

"Hi, Mr. Kennedy," Ty said as Dad came around the corner into the room.

"Tyler," my dad responded, nodding. His eyes were on the materials scattered across the coffee table and Ty's crooked foundation. "I thought maybe I could give the two of you a hand." He rubbed his hands together. By the look of him, we wouldn't be doing any of our own work that afternoon—not that I was complaining.

The basement door opened again.

"Roger, may I speak with you for a moment?" Mom called.

Dad left and we heard him clomp up the stairs. The basement door closed.

"What are you going to do about it?" Ty said, picking up our conversation from the day before.

"About what?" Maybe if I pretended like I didn't know what he meant, he'd stop talking about it.

Ty glared at me from under his bangs. "English. You can't hide from it forever."

"I'll just read the part," I said, irritated. "I'll pretend—follow along in the book with my finger and talk slow if I have to. It's no big deal."

"If that's what you need to think, that's fine by me. But you could just read the way you did the other day and see what happens."

Before I could ask him what he meant by *that*, the door opened for the third time. Dad came downstairs with the spark missing from his eye, less exuberant than before. Behind him were Ely and Judith, each carrying a shopping bag of what I guessed were more supplies.

"Hey," I said. They sat down with Ty and me while my dad hovered around the coffee table, waiting for everyone to get comfortable.

"How about I show you four some other versions of the Globe?" he said.

Something was not right.

"Aren't you going to help us with ours?" He was staring at the supplies with the same intensity that a starving person looks at Thanksgiving dinner.

"I think it's best if you do this yourself," he said, and sighed. Mom must have told him to back off, afraid that he'd take over our assignment. She was probably right, but still.

We cleared off the coffee table according to his directions, and he disappeared into his office. Shuffling, banging, and a muffled "raven's feathers!" curse came through the wall. Judith giggled behind a cupped hand. Ty nudged her.

"Think that's funny? You should hear what he says when he's *really* mad," he whispered. That sent Judith into more giggles. I stuck my tongue out at both of them.

"It is a little messy in here," Dad called. "No need to be alarmed."

He emerged carrying a Globe on a piece of heavy cardboard.

"This one I carved out of Styrofoam," he said, eyes shining again. "It took me all of August to get the seats right." He pointed out the dimensions, the setup of the stage, where the entrances and exits were, and how he'd used toothpicks to reinforce the tiers between the second and third levels. Then he brought out one he made using Popsicle sticks. And the corrugated cardboard version. He gave us the guided tour of each.

By our third detailed discussion of the "tiring house," Ty was slumped over, a dazed expression on his face. I was nearly asleep. Ely's dreads drooped, and Judith, I was pretty sure, was composing music in her head. She'd hum every so often, and run her fingers on her thigh like she was playing piano.

"Dad," I interrupted, shaking myself out of my stupor, "we really need to get started on ours." I hoped he wouldn't be offended.

"Of course!" he said. "As Willie says, pleasure and action make the hours seem short." When none of us responded, he kept going. "But I do want to share my favorite of the collection . . ." He disappeared into his office for the final time, thankfully—he didn't have any more left after this one.

The last Globe was mounted on a piece of wood— maybe plywood? It was the most beautiful of all of them. Painted a rich shade of brown, with real stage curtains and tiny details on the seats and entrances, it had clearly taken him a long time to complete. Ty sat straight up again.

"Whoa," Ely breathed.

Dad nodded. "I made this one out of leftover shingles from when we had the house redone. It was the first one."

"It's amazing," Judith agreed.

After show-and-tell, Dad went over the directions with us.

"Well," he said when he was done, "I guess I should let you work now." I could tell he wanted to stay and help, but Mom would be mad if he did. He started putting the Globes back in his office.

I thought I knew what might make him feel better. "Could you leave one for us to look at?" I asked. Ty nodded his head.

"Yeah—I mean, yes," he agreed, forgetting that it's my mom who gets hung up on the grammar thing.

"It would really help us know if we were doing it right."

"A wonderful idea!" Dad said, smile returning. "I shall leave you with this one." He put the shingle Globe on an end table next to the couch. "May it inspire you to greatness." He gave a half bow and went back upstairs.

"Well," said Ty, after a glance at his watch, "*that* took an hour and a half. We'd better get started."

We laid our materials out and got to work.

"I'm guessing the two of you already hashed out the English thing, huh?" said Judith. She laid a piece of wood onto their foundation and held her hand out for the glue.

Ty nodded. "Ham wants to fake-read next time."

"That's so bogus," Judith said. She shook her head, sending her streaky red hair flying. She'd dyed it again.

"Why shouldn't I read like everyone else? It'd get Wimple off my case," I complained.

"Never deny your true nature." Ely used his *Star Wars* voice: deep and slow. I hucked a piece of balsa wood at him. It wasn't satisfying—just flitted in the air and landed on the table.

"This *is* my true nature: no Shakespeare, terrible at algebra—"

"Perpetual crush on Carter Teegan," Judith teased. I glared at her. "Ooooh, do you think he was the one who left—?"

I cut her off quickly and gave her a little kick under the table. I still had no plans to share my pig mystery with either of them. "That is *not* what I was going to say!"

"But it's true," she said.

Ty snapped a piece of wood in half. "He's an idiot," he muttered. "I don't know why you waste your time."

"Why is this all about me?" I cried. "Don't you people have any drama to deal with?" I was only half kidding. All of a sudden, I felt attacked in my own house. It was a new, and unsettling, feeling.

"Chill, yo," Ely directed at Ty and Judith, "or Ham is going to climb into that suit of armor and go medieval on us." I cracked a smile.

That broke the tension, and I think the others realized that talking about any of my issues wasn't going to get them anywhere. Instead, our talk shifted to a songwriting contest Judith wanted to enter and how Ty and Ely scored tickets to the last regular season Red Sox game, thanks to Ely's uncle, who worked for the team.

By the time they went home, we'd set up the foundation and stage level of our theaters. The theater Ty and I made was constructed from the balsa wood. Learning something from Dad's agonizing lecture, we planned to use a cardboard/Styrofoam combo to build the upper levels.

"Nicely done," Dad said when he came down to check it out after dinner. "Have you decided what scene you will stage yet?"

I shook my head.

"Not a decision to be taken lightly," he said, mistaking my lack of consideration for indecision. If it weren't for Ty's suggestion to work on it, I probably wouldn't have started.

"I'm thinking of using LEGO people as the characters," I said, trying to distract him.

"Speak ye no of such heresy!" He spun toward me.

Well, he was distracted all right. "No players of the Bard's work shall be represented by an infant's *figurines.*" He said the last word as though it tasted like spoiled milk.

"Well, what should I use?"

"Something noble! Something that is worthy of the representation." He rubbed his chin. "I have just the thing." He disappeared into his office and came back with a book, which is how I found myself cutting fancy illustrations out of a collection of sonnets ("I have a second copy, and it's for a worthy cause," my father admitted) and mounting them to cardboard to serve as my players, cursing Mrs. Wimple and Mr. Hoffstedder in my head the whole time.

While I dissected the pictures, I couldn't help but think about what Ty said about acting. It *would* be kind of cool to have something I was good at, but why did it have to be this? It was difficult enough to get my parents to chill out and join the twenty-first century. This could set us all back by a few hundred years.

Sunday night, I sat in my room, copy of *A Midsummer Night's Dream* propped open on my knees. Mom, Dad, and Dezzie were out at a lecture. After all the talk about Shakespeare and Globes this weekend, it was the perfect time to test out Mrs. Wimple's theory that my Shakespeare-spouting was a "gift" and not an accident.

I opened it randomly to the end of Act II. Helena, Hermia, and Lysander were fighting. I picked Helena's lines:

"Wherefore was I to this keen mockery born?/When at your hands did I deserve this scorn?/Is't not enough, is't not enough, young man,/That I did never, no, nor never can,/Deserve a sweet look from Demetrius' eye,/But you must flout my insufficiency?" It was easy—the phrases came out of me as naturally as talking to friends. I tried another one from the same scene, this time with Lysander speaking:

"For as a surfeit of the sweetest things/The deepest loathing to the stomach brings,/Or as tie heresies that men do leave/Are hated most of those they did deceive,/

So thou, my surfeit and my heresy,/Of all be hated, but the most of me!" Again, same thing. Even though I didn't know the meaning of some of the words, I was pretty sure I was pronouncing them right. And my voice had fallen into the rhythm of the poetry. Truthfully, it was kind of fun. I knew how the characters were feeling and could sense the emotion Shakespeare built into the words. But, really, *why* did it have to be Shakespeare-reading that I was good at? Couldn't it have been something useful, like cooking contemporary recipes? Or exciting and dangerous, like tightrope walking?

Silly questions aside, how would this impact the Dezzie situation at school? Already my parents were way more involved in my life since she entered HoHo. And that made me think of the Salute to Shakespeare extravaganza. I'd been afraid to ask if Mom had called Mrs. Wimple or Mr. Hoffstedder, choosing instead to live in terror that one of them would show up wearing an Elizabethan collar or Tudor jumper when I least expected it. There was no way I was telling them about this freaky talent.

It was sure proving to be more of a curse than a gift.

ꞈXi꞊

The following week in art, Saber and Mauri, who were in a different history/English block from me, brought up the dreaded projects after finishing a long, boring conversation about some ski trip Mauri's dad was going to take them on over winter break.

"Mrs. Wimple is making us act *Midsummer's Night's Dream* out in class," said Saber, as if Dezzie didn't already know that. She splattered green paint on her canvas. We were making Pollock paintings. I didn't think that Pollock would like her hot pink and lime color choices, but it wasn't my place to say anything. Evidently, Dezzie didn't agree.

"Pollock's palette was much more muted overall," she said, mixing a gray/green shade. "He was reflecting post-WWII angst. And it's mid-*summer*, not midsummer's," she added.

I kicked her chair, both in an effort to remind her of the "blending in" rules and to stop any Shakespeare-reading talk. Immediately, her face turned pink.

"So?" asked Mauri.

"You're not being true to the abstract expressionist way of thought," Dezzie explained. "Really, your palette should be more elemental and basic." I gave up.

Saber looked uncomfortable. "But these are my favorite colors," she whined.

Why did Saber care what Dezzie thought? I was working with deep blues and black, but that was because those were my favorite colors too.

"It's, you know, personal *choice*," Mauri piped in. "It's *art*."

Worried that Dezzie might lecture them on the nature of artistic expression, I tried to change the subject. "How's the play?" I asked, realizing that I'd brought up the one subject I wanted to avoid. I stabbed my frustration at the canvas.

"It's so fun," said Mauri. "Today I got to read Hippolyta's lines. She was queen of the Amazons, you know." I didn't want to tell her that she'd also been kidnapped and forced to marry Theseus. Better to let Mauri think of her as a regular, royal queen, so she could enjoy acting all princessy—and so it wouldn't draw attention to our Shakespeare experience. At least she wasn't questioning me or Dezzie.

"Hippolyta's such a good representation of Shakespeare's feelings of the female as slave," said Dezzie. She was struggling with her painting and not paying *any* attention to her rules. "It just doesn't look *right*," she muttered.

Mauri and Saber gave her matching blank stares. "Shakespeare's what?" Saber asked.

I glared at Dezzie and tried to deflect the conversation. "You know, all the women have to ask for permission to do stuff, instead of making their own choices."

"I thought she was cool," said Mauri. She stuck out her lower lip.

"I like your painting," I said, hoping she'd let me change the subject. If they realized that Dezzie was making them look dumb, I'd have to deal with their embarrassment and annoyance for the rest of the day. Mauri was using browns and oranges. Our goal was to capture a specific emotion on canvas. Hers was called "Bored."

"Thanks," she said.

Dezzie smacked her brush on the table, sending out a short dark green spray from the bristles and making us jump. Her face was red.

"I hate this," she said, scowling at her easel. I moved around her to look.

The title of her painting was "Understanding." She was using shades of green, gray, and blue. We were supposed to be splattering and dribbling the paint on the canvas, but her splatters were intermingled with smears and strokes.

"It looks fine to me," I said, studying it. It was like anyone else's painting in the class: The colors dripped and swirled together, and splashes dotted the whole thing.

"It's *not* fine," Dezzie snapped. "I can't get it to look the way I want it to." She crossed her arms.

"What's all the discussion over here?" Ms. Finch-Bean walked around Dezzie's easel. "This is good, Desdemona," she said. "You've chosen a strong color palette."

"But it doesn't look right," insisted Dezzie. "Not like it does in my head."

Ms. Finch-Bean started talking to her about trying your best, and how art is an evolution, but Dezzie's gray eyes just grew darker. I could tell that no matter what the teacher told her, she wouldn't be happy with her work. I'd never seen Dezzie act like that before. She was always good at anything she tried.

Mauri and Saber, although pretending to paint, were obviously listening to the conversation. Mauri wrote something on a piece of notebook paper and slipped it into her book bag when she thought I wasn't looking.

When she was done with Desdemona, Ms. Finch-Bean gave each of us at the table a quick review—she suggested that I add more dark purple to my piece—and then clapped her hands to get our attention.

"I have an announcement," she said. "When we're done with our Pollock paintings, they'll be hung in the halls for everyone to enjoy!"

She went on to explain that parents, teachers, and

administrators were looking forward to seeing the work . . . all the typical stuff.

Dezzie pouted and didn't say another word for the rest of class.

After art, she didn't want me to walk her upstairs. "I *know* where choir is," she hissed, an irritable tone creeping into her voice. "I've been going there for weeks now." She swung her backpack over her shoulders and stalked out of the art room.

Fine by me. I could use being early for English. But as I walked—not ran—to my class, I felt strange. Walking around with Dezzie was weird, but now it was just as weird to be without her.

Later on, I thought I'd try and find Dezzie at choir before she went to TLC and see if her mood had improved. But when I got downstairs, Mrs. Applebaum said that she'd already left, with two other girls. The back of my neck prickled.

"Was it Mauri Lee and Saber Greene, by any chance?" I asked her. She raised her eyebrows at me.

"How did you know?"

My heart sank a little.

"I just guessed."

I didn't have time to make it from there to TLC and pre-algebra before the late bell, so checking on Dezzie would have to wait. The whole time Mr. Symphony talked about x and y as components of a problem, all I could think about were Mauri and Saber. What did they want with my sister?

The class ended, and I realized I hadn't even written down the homework assignment, let alone taken notes. Scribbling it down from the board, I packed my stuff and tried to catch Dezzie one more time.

I wouldn't make it to The Learning Center before she left, so instead I went straight to the front office, where Mom would be picking her up. As I came around the corner, I spotted Mom at the end of the hall, brown and gray bun bobbing above the kids' heads. She was wearing her favorite red cloak—the one with the bells sewn into the front seams. The passing kids shot smirks, chuckles, and funny glances at her.

I stopped so sharply I nearly stepped out of my sneakers. Was it was worth being stared at to approach them and talk to Dezzie? As I weighed my options, Mom moved to one side to avoid a student. She was speaking with someone. Someone short. And then I realized it wasn't Dezzie. Dezzie was standing next to her and still wearing a grouchy expression.

My mother was talking to another girl. My mother was talking to Saber Greene.

☙ Xii ☙

he urge to run as fast as I could in the opposite direction came over me, and I nearly gave in. I even turned around.

What stopped me?

I was too far away for them to notice me in the crush of kids going to lunch. But the hall would empty in another minute, so my spying couldn't last long. I maneuvered to one side and stood against a row of lockers, head down, peeking at them through a curtain of my hair.

Mom had a huge smile on her face, and was nodding like her head was on a spring at whatever Saber was saying. Saber wore an expression I'd seen many times in class—round eyes, a big smile, face tilted up like she was really interested in the other person—but as soon as the teacher turned his or her back, that face would disappear and a nasty one would take its place. As soon as Mom and Dezzie left, I knew that sneer would appear and whom her lunch conversation would be about—and how funny it would sound to the others at her table.

The crowd in the hall thinned. Should I walk over

there, or leave? I needed to make a quick decision, but my feet felt as though they were stapled to the floor. They'd see me soon.

Saber nodded at my mother again, and smiled so wide I was sure the top of her head was going to fall off. I kind of hoped it would.

It didn't. She smiled and waved at Dezzie too. My mother, in her typical fashion, curtsied her good-bye. Was it possible that Saber's mouth stretched just a tiny bit wider? She obviously remembered Mom from the Ren Faire. Dezzie and Mom turned to leave, and Saber watched, smile shrinking faster than one of Mom's wool sweaters in the dryer.

I edged away from the locker and went to the caf. My emotions were as clear as a Pollock painting—a puddle of anger at Saber for mocking my mom, a splash of irritation with Dezzie for being at HoHo to begin with, dribbles of frustration with my mother, her crazy habits, and what would happen if she knew if I could "perform"—everything combined into a messy soup of mad.

Ty, Ely, and Judith didn't even ask where I had been when I plopped into my seat—since Dezzie showed up, they were used to me being late for everything. I tossed my lunch bag on the table, scowling at it. Saber was a jerk, and I didn't know what to do about it.

"Hey Ham-let." Her sickly sweet voice was behind me. I turned, along with Ty, Ely, and everyone else at our table.

"I saw your mom today, when she came to pick up your sister." Saber said "mom" and "sister" like the words were full of lead—slow and heavy. "It was nice to talk to her. About old times."

I didn't speak. If I said something mean, she would use it to mock me somehow. Instead, I bit the inside of my cheek and tried to keep my temper under control. When she saw I wasn't planning to respond, she continued.

"I really liked her cloak," she said. "Did she leave her Maypole at home?" I bit down harder to keep my mouth from getting ahead of my brain. In a second, I'd be able to taste blood.

"What do you want?" Ty barked at her. He sat straight as the deck of his skateboard, clutching the back of his chair with both hands.

Saber shrugged. "Just thought I'd let Ham-let know that her mother is very excited to help with our Shake-speare project." She kept her face friendly and neutral, like she was giving us the algebra homework, but it was a mask.

"Really? She *is*? That is *such* news to me. Wowzers, Saber, you are totally an investigative reporter." Ely oozed sarcasm from the roots of his dreds. Scowling, Saber flounced from our table.

"Sweet!" Judith cheered, and Ely high-fived across the table.

"Thanks, guys," I muttered, happy for the help, but

embarrassed that I needed backup to clear Saber from our presence. Ty and Ely began dissecting her reaction and his performance.

"Dude, what was she talking about?" Judith asked me, too low for the boys to hear. "Is your mom really coming in to help?" I shook my head.

Some things aren't worth explaining. And besides, if Saber was right, Judith would find out for herself soon enough.

ᴄXiiiᴖ

When I got home, I found out just how soon that might be.

"I met a girl in one of your classes today," Mom said over dinner. "Savor, I think her name was? She remembered me from a Faire we did two years ago."

Dezzie stared straight at her food, acting like she wasn't at the dinner table. Dad was deep into another stack of sonnets. He barely touched the Cornish hen cooling on his plate. Iago sat in the corner on his purple velvet pillow, waiting for us to finish so he could get scraps—stir-fried in seventeenth-century gravy, of course.

I had no choice but to answer.

"Saber," I replied.

"Correct. She escorted your sister to the office before lunchtime. Was that not nice of her?"

When she realized I wasn't going to respond, she went on. "We spoke about the Salute to Shakespeare unit your class is doing. She is very excited."

"Mmm-hmmm," I said, putting a forkful of mashed potatoes into my mouth. The less I said, the better off I'd be—I didn't want Mom to know that I a.) didn't like Saber and b.) hadn't actually said anything to my teachers about her offer to help.

"She gave me the names of your teachers, as you seem to have forgotten to contact them on our behalf. She seemed to think they would like having us involved. What do you think, Hamlet?" The look on her face read: "Why did not you give us their names?"

I nearly choked. "She did? Really?"

"I think that is wonderful," Dad said, finally surfacing from his stack of work. Iago also perked up. "There is much we can both offer, Prudence." Their faces were mirrors of Elizabethan joy.

"I shall call Mrs. Wimple tomorrow," Mom said.

Dezzie gave me a quizzical look. I guess the horror I felt on the inside was presenting itself all over my face.

I sunk lower in my seat. First Desdemona, then the English/history class, my reading "talent," and now my parents—eighth grade was turning into a Salute to Shakespeare, all right. Only the type of salute I wanted to give the Bard would have gotten me in big, big trouble.

After dinner I went to my room, to tackle my pre-algebra homework, followed by Iago. He's an ex–show dog and the most picky animal I've ever met. He'll only lie on the bed if the sheets smell clean, and refuses to do any "business" unless it's behind the rosebush in our backyard. As I went through my bag, searching for my assignment notebook, he hopped onto my bed and gave the comforter and pillow a thorough sniff. Deciding that it wasn't quite right, he jumped down and sat in front of my bedroom door, sighing until I let him out.

"Fine."

I flopped onto my comforter—the sheets were fresh enough for me—and stared at the ceiling. There was no avoiding it: My parents would be involved with my classes in some way, at some point, this term. And they'd find out about what happened in English.

I'd succeeded in both not reading aloud in class and not thinking about what happened outside of class for the past few days. But it hadn't made anything go away.

I *hated* Shakespeare. He was responsible for ruining my life. And as far as I was concerned, being able to read his words was no gift. It was just another thing that made me different—what I wanted to avoid at all costs. Dad was always talking about the way people acted in public versus in private—one way was how you were, the other was how you behaved. Of course he had a Shakespeare quote to explain it: "God has given you one face, and you make yourself another."

The face I'd make wouldn't involve any of this stuff.

I dug my pre-al book from my bag and stared at the same graph problem for fifteen minutes. It did not improve my mood. We had a test coming up soon, and I couldn't figure out where x and y were supposed to go, or what they were supposed to do when they got there. I read the beginning of the chapter, then reread it, hoping that the words would mean something the second time through. No luck.

I tried reading the end of the chapter, but the "helpful hints" weren't so helpful if you had no idea what they were referring to. Since I'd been preoccupied trying to figure out what to do with Dezzie, I didn't have any notes from class, either.

A check of the clock. I'd been working on pre-al for forty-five minutes, and was no better off than when I started. I sighed, then dropped my forehead to my desk. There was no option left.

Dragging my feet the whole way, I went down the hall and knocked on my sister's door. Usually I had no problem asking Dezzie for help, but after dealing with Saber and being wrapped in Mom and Dad's educational cloak, all because of her, I was in no rush for assistance.

"Come in," Dezzie said. Her voice sounded strange—kind of like when she had a cold or bad allergies, but I went in anyway.

I liked visiting her room. Everything was always neat and put away, unlike the tangled piles of clothes and books and notebooks that littered my floor. Instead of the action movie posters and collages of my friends hanging on my walls, her room was decorated with a poster of the periodic table of the elements, which she'd memorized at four and a half (why leave it up if you know everything on it?), a chart of the U.S. presidents, and "for a touch of whimsy," as she said, there was a mobile in the corner dangling symbols of famous novelists—a raven for Edgar Allan Poe, a red letter A for Nathaniel Hawthorne, a ghost for Dickens, and, of course, a quill pen for you-know-who. She'd made it at SMARTS two years ago.

Instead of sitting at her desk, books open and computer on, Dezzie was facedown on the bed, head stuffed under her pillow. Only the back of her shirt and her Care Bears pajama pants were visible. Iago was stretched out at her feet, snoozing. Not an open book in sight. I stopped.

"Dez, are you okay?" The dog opened one eye and gave me a dirty look.

"Fine," came her little voice, muffled by the pillows. "What do you need?"

I slipped my math book and notebook on the bureau next to her bed. "Um, I was going to ask you for help with pre-algebra," I said. "I can come back later, if you want." I'd never seen her like this. Iago, sleep disturbed, stretched and hopped down. He trotted to the door and gave me another annoyed look before leaving.

"That would be fine." It seemed like the pillow was the one doing the talking. "Congratulations on your stellar reading in English, by the way." Then a sniffle. Pillows don't sniffle.

"Uh, thanks?" I said, hoping she wouldn't tell Mom and Dad and wondering where she heard about it, anyway. "Are you *sure* you're okay?" I took a step closer to her bed.

"I said I'm *fine!*" she said, much louder this time. I froze. "Just *get out!*" She made this funny gasping noise.

I didn't move. I could tell she was crying, and probably had been since before I came in, but I didn't know why, or what to do about it.

Dezzie's not a crier. Even when she was a little baby, she rarely cried. She didn't throw temper tantrums when she was two or three, like Ty's little brother—instead, in a calm voice, she would explain that she wanted to read *that* specific textbook or would ask someone to hold her so she could better see *that* museum piece. I'm the one who's always battling emotions.

"Do you want to talk about it?" I tried. I stepped closer to the bed.

Silence. Maybe that was a good sign. I perched on the edge, barely putting any weight on the mattress.

Her head popped up from between the pillows. Her round face was covered with big red splotches, curly hair sticking to her forehead in sweaty clumps. She chewed on her lower lip, and her eyes were puffy and pink around the edges. Dezzie, I was both surprised and pleased to see, looked like me when she cried—like a regular, angry, upset kid. I tried not to smile.

"What's wrong?" I said, using a soft voice.

Her eyes filled with tears. That's when I noticed that she was clutching Curie, her stuffed rabbit. Curie had been her favorite toy before she learned to read, and sat on a shelf over her desk. It was one of the only "baby" things that Dezzie would allow in her room. As far as I knew, Curie had been sitting in the same spot for nearly six years. This was bad.

"I–I–hate school!" she blurted. The tears overflowed, spilling down her cheeks and dripping off her chin into her lap.

"You could ask Mom and Dad to change your curriculum," I began. The expression she made would have melted a stone.

"Not *that* school," she said. "HoHo."

"You hate HoHo?"

I was confused. What was there to hate about HoHo? Besides all the usual stuff–teachers, homework, annoying people–it was just *school.* No one *loved* it, but it's what you had to do. It was normal.

Normal, I guess, if you'd been going for eight years.

That's when I realized I'd been in school longer than Dezzie had been alive. Even with the "lessons" I'd given her, she had no idea what to do there. And even with her brains, she was still only seven. I hadn't realized how hard it would be for her. I put my hand on her shoulder to try and comfort her.

"I hate it," she repeated. Her face was turning back to its regular color. It seemed like the crying was gone for now. I relaxed.

"What do you hate?" I removed my hand, crossed my legs on the bed and faced her.

"I can't *do* it," said Dezzie.

"Do what? I know that the desks and lockers are tall, but I thought they took care of that in—"

She shook her head, cutting me off. "It's not the desks. I can't do the work. Art, to be more specific. And they are going to hang the Pollock paintings for everyone to see." She stared straight at the floor when she said this.

"You hate school because you can't paint?"

That was it? I guess my voice sounded more incredulous than it should have. I mean, I was worried that she was stressing over all these changes, and she was upset because she couldn't do *art?* It was almost funny—I was worried because I was performing too well, she was upset because she couldn't stand out the way she was used to. She flopped backward onto the pillow and hid her face again.

"Just go," she said. "I knew you couldn't understand."

Now, if she had said any other word but "couldn't," I probably *would* have gotten up and left. But after everything I'd been going through recently, there was no way I was going to let her suggest that I didn't understand why she was upset because I wasn't smart enough. I stood up, boiling. There was no stopping what came next.

"Just because you're the brains around here doesn't mean other people are too stupid to understand stuff," I sputtered. "Too bad that you can't do everything perfect on the first try. Welcome to life. *Average* life." I picked up my pre-algebra book and notebook and stormed out, slamming the door behind me.

Right before it closed, I saw Dezzie's tear-streaked face, eyes the size of saucers, shocked that I could say something so mean.

So was I.

Eighth grade, thus far:

* My genius sister is ruining my life
* Saber and Mauri are stalking her—and me
* I'm tanking pre-al
* A mystery person is leaving origami pigs in my locker
* Carter is still not interested in me. *At all.*
* I have a horrible, unwanted "talent"
* And my parents are probably going to come to school to humiliate me in public

If these are the highlights, I'm in big trouble.

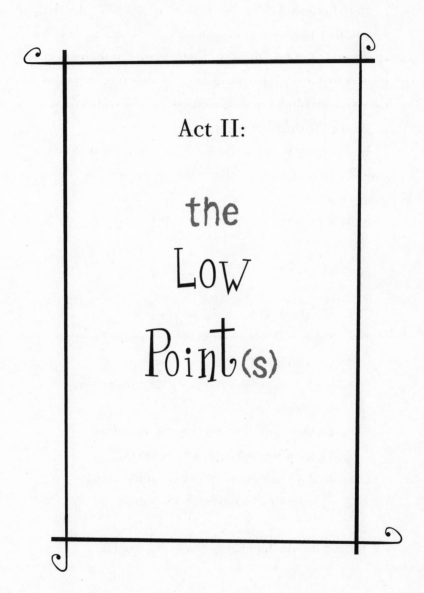

Act II:

the

Low

Point(s)

1

T he next few mornings followed the same uncomfortable routine: Dezzie and I ate breakfast in silence, then suffered through Mom's wild rides to school without a word. Mom doesn't like cars—excuse me, *does not*—and as a result, is a terrible driver.

"Driving does not allow me to do anything *else*," she explained to Ty's mother once. "I need that time to think and read and grade." Therefore, she drives like she *is* somewhere else—slamming on the brakes at stop signs, jerking into traffic to make turns. It's terrifying. Even Dezzie can't read in the car when Mom is behind the wheel, and Mom had been insisting that she bring us to school "until Desdemona gets acclimated to her surroundings." Thankfully, HoHo is only four streets away from our house. But, seriously, we'd all be better off if she could ride around in a horse and carriage, a la 1599.

Because of our fight, I'd stopped escorting Dezzie around the building. We still had to sit at the same table in art, but she only spoke to Mauri and Saber. They didn't seem to notice our silence—or if they did, they didn't say anything about it in front of me.

It was probably because they were too busy being Dezzie's new best friends. The change in how they treated her was so gradual, I almost didn't notice it. Then one day, it was as vibrant as Mauri's purple nail polish—and the matching purple origami pig in my locker, the origins of which were still unknown. Judith wanted to "stake out" my locker to see who was leaving them, but since they didn't appear with any consistency, we decided it'd be a waste of our time. Her other suggestion—leaving the folding fiend a note—made me too nervous. What would I write? *Are thine intentions true? Reveal thyself, oh villain of my heart!* Uh, no. I decided to just wait and let the mystery unfold while the misery of eighth grade steamrolled on.

The Scene: *Art class, post-fight.*
Mauri: Dezzie, I love your shirt!
Dezzie (looking down at her white tee with floral embroidery at the hem): Thank you.
Saber: It's so *cute! Such* a DIY project.
Mauri: Yeah. And that joke you told last period was so funny. Can you tell it again?
Dezzie: Knock, knock.
Saber: Who's there?

Dezzie (using a joke my dad told once a month at dinner): Old lady!

Mauri: Old lady who?

Dezzie: I didn't know you could yodel!

Saber and Mauri laugh like it's the funniest thing they've ever heard. I scowl at my painting.

Dezzie: Shakespeare invented the knock-knock joke.

Mauri: Really?

Dezzie: Some people think so. In act two, scene three of *Macbeth* . . .

It was nauseating.

Everything she did or said, they thought was the most wonderful, funniest, smartest . . . *whatever.* Dezzie ate it up. She giggled at their jokes and started tossing her hair like them, staring at me when she did. She was trying to get to me.

I had to remind myself that I gave her the stupid rules about blending in in the first place. Saber and Mauri even stopped making those weird side glances to each other whenever Dezzie went off on one of her educational tangents. In fact, they were encouraging her to talk about school even *more* by talking about it themselves.

"What's up with Hermia and Helena in the play?"

Saber asked one day as we were finishing our Pollock paintings. She dabbed more lime green on her canvas. I splattered some gray on mine to look like I was working, but my mind was on the ever-growing collection of pigs in my locker. There were four in there now. Soon I'd have a full-fledged sounder (a fancy word for a collection of pigs. Dezzie taught me that one years ago, when she went on a "collective nouns" memorizing binge). But I was nowhere closer to finding out who was sneaking them into the vent.

"What do you mean?" Dezzie said. She scowled at her piece. She'd basically stopped painting over the past few classes; just dabbed a color here and there to seem busy.

I was still holding a shred of hope that Carter might be my crafty locker stalker, but it was a small shred. The boy paid more attention to his collection of sneakers than to me—most of them color-coordinated to match his shirts.

"Well, they're friends, right?" Dezzie nodded. Saber went on, "But when Dmitri and Lysol—"

"Demetrius and Lysander," Dezzie corrected.

"Whatever. When they both start liking Helena, Hermia gets mad at *her*. And they get in this huge fight. It's not Helena's fault that they like her."

Whoa. Saber's questions sounded like the homework assignment Mrs. Wimple gave us on character relationships in the play. A *lot* like the assignment. Now it was me who only pretended to paint.

"Helena thinks that they're playing a mean joke on her," Dezzie said.

Wait, I thought, concentration derailed by Dezzie's comment, were my pigs a joke too? Did someone think it was funny? It was a possibility I didn't want to consider. Lately, those pigs were the only part of school I looked forward to.

Dezzie seemed happy to put her brush down and talk about *Midsummer*. Mauri put her brush down too. I couldn't see what she was doing behind her easel, but you didn't need a genius IQ to figure it out once the sound of rustling papers reached our ears.

"She thinks that the boys are pretending to like her because Hermia told them to, especially because they changed their minds about her so fast." Dezzie went on for a few more minutes, explaining stuff about perception and reality. Saber and Mauri listened to every word, not interrupting her at all. I started painting again, but paid attention the entire time. Their conversation gave me a tight feeling in the pit of my stomach. Mauri and Saber were using Dezzie for her brains.

"Hey Dezzie," said Mauri at the end of class—that was another thing I didn't like. Up until she'd started HoHo, I was the only one who called her Dezzie. "Can you stay for lunch one day? Saber and I think you should totally sit at our table with us. It'd be fun."

The cup of brushes I'd rinsed slipped out of my hand

and clattered to the floor, spraying pale beads of red, blue, and gray water all over the easel and table and, I was sad to see, my white capris. I almost didn't care, though. After milking her for the homework, had Saber and Mauri just invited my sister to sit at their lunch table?

"I could ask," Dezzie answered, a pleased little smile dancing at the corner of her lips. Grrrr.

"Hey, bacon fingers," Saber said, "make sure you don't miss any spots when you clean up."

"Absolutely, Your Highness," I muttered.

Clenching my teeth so I wouldn't say anything else that could get me in trouble, I bent over the mess and stuffed the spilled brushes back into the cup. A familiar giggle tinkled down to me. Dezzie. Laughing at Saber's comment! I chomped on the inside of my cheek to keep from throwing the cup at her.

My genius sister had turned into an idiot.

I stomped up to English, seething.

"Perfect timing, Ms. Kennedy," Mrs. Wimple said as I entered. "I was just about to tell the class about our Salute to Shakespeare performance."

I slid into my seat, more annoyed now than when I'd left art. Ty raised an eyebrow at me, and I gave him a quick shake of my head. I'd explain my scowl later.

"We will be performing select scenes from *A Midsummer Night's Dream* in front of an audience," Mrs. Wimple continued. She brought her hands to her chest in two excited fists—the same gesture my mom made when talking about the Bard. I nearly groaned out loud. "I have prepared a master cast list," she went on, "and shall now reveal your parts." She began reading from a sheet of paper.

"KC Rails, set design," she announced. KC gave a wicked grin.

"Tyler Spencer, Theseus." Across the aisle, I saw his face go pale.

"Hamlet Kennedy, Puck," she said.

I knew it.

She went on, going through the whole class, and I stopped listening. Thankfully, she didn't assign me a part to read today, so I just sat and stewed, fretting over the latest blow to my eighth-grade year.

Finally, the bell rang.

"A word, Ms. Kennedy." Mrs. Wimple's sharp tone cut through the clatter.

Ty glanced at me. "Good luck," he mouthed, and scooted off to his next class.

I dragged my feet up to the teacher's desk, where she was shuffling through our homework.

"Mrs. Wimple, I shouldn't be late—" She cut me off with a wave.

"Despite your obvious reluctance, you will play the part of Puck in our performance. And play it well." She knew I was going to complain about her selection. She lifted her hand, gesturing toward the door. The she sat back in her chair and pulled a stack of papers toward her. She didn't look at me again.

Struggling between shame and anger, I stood there for a second or two—it felt like fifteen years—not knowing what to do. She coughed, which broke me from my shocked trance. I bolted from the room.

I'd have to *perform*. In front of people. That thought, plus everything that had happened in art, put me over the edge.

This time, I didn't even make it to the bathroom.

Only a few feet from the classroom, someone swapped lead for my legs and I had to stop and lean against a wall. Tears burned my eyes, and the posters and signs promoting the afternoon's soccer match and band concert blurred like a tie-dyed shirt.

It was getting harder and harder to hold back the flood building in my eyes. I rubbed my face with my hands, and forced myself in the direction of the nearest girls' room. Not even one month into school, and I'd already broken down more times than I had in the previous two years. Some cold water helped, but it didn't wash away the feeling of dread that had settled in my chest.

When I walked into Mr. Symphony's room, one of the student messengers from the front office was standing next to his desk, delivering an office call slip. On his way out he gave me a "you're heading to the office" look.

"Miss Kennedy, I'd like to speak with you for a moment," Mr. S. began, the green call slip pinched between his fingers. "The rest of you, please study the beginning of chapter three. We will get started momentarily."

Fear bounced through my body. Had I done anything wrong? Ely glanced at me and I gave him a half shrug. I had no idea what this was about.

Mouth dry, I stood at Mr. Symphony's desk.

"Dr. Lafevre would like to see you," he said, handing me the slip. "You may take your belongings with you, but if this consultation ends before the period I expect you back here immediately. We are doing a review session for our first test."

"Sure," I croaked, and took the pale green piece of paper. I had no idea who Dr. Lafevre was, but I didn't want to ask Mr. S. in front of the whole class in case I didn't like the answer.

In the hall, I glanced at the slip:

Send student to: James Lafevre

When: Immediately

For: Consultation

Then I remembered—James, Ely's counselor friend, was Dr. Lafevre. I was being sent to the school counselor?!

The whole walk from pre-al to the administrative suites I tried to figure out why. Had something happened? Were Mom and Dad okay? Had there been an accident? Were they being held hostage by a rival Ren

Faire troupe? Had something happened to Dezzie on her walk to class? Just about every possible scenario blew through my head.

By the time I reached Dr. Lafevre's door, I was convinced that it was bad news. Sweat ran down my back, and my legs were wobbly jelly-filled balloons.

The door opened and a student I didn't recognize slipped out. He kept his eyes on the floor as he passed me.

"Hamlet Kennedy? You out there?" A deep voice came from inside the office.

"Uh-huh," I whispered, then cleared my throat.

"Well, come on in. I don't bite." The door opened wider, and I got a look at Dr. Lafevre, whom I hadn't seen since sixth-grade orientation.

Tall—really tall—and skinny, he had a short brown beard and long brownish-blond hair pulled back into a ponytail. He also had a nice smile and crinkly blue eyes.

"Everything with your family is okay," he said as soon as he saw me. "No worries."

I let out a huge breath.

"I make sure that's the first thing I say when someone new comes to the door. Well, that and call me James." He gestured to his office. "Come in and have a seat."

I stepped into his office. Instead of a big desk, he had a small one stuck in a corner. Two bulgy green armchairs squatted in the middle of the room, a teeny coffee table covered in pamphlets in between them.

James sat in one of the chairs and offered me the other one. I put my bag on the floor and tried to perch on the edge of the seat, but the chair was too squashy and I fell into it. I struggled to sit up straight.

"So," he said, propping his hands on his knees and leaning toward me. He was so lanky that sitting that way he looked like a coat hanger that'd been bent in half. "I bet you're wondering why you're here and not in math class."

I nodded.

"I hear that you have a lot going on right now," he said, "and I thought you might want to talk about it."

A completely clueless "huh?" came out of my mouth, but my brain buzzed with a zillion questions and emotions: Who had told him I "had a lot going on"? What did he know? Was this about Dezzie? About English? About Saber and Mauri using my sister? About my plummeting math grade? What was I supposed to say? I was embarrassed, angry, and confused, all at once.

He leaned back in his chair and crossed his legs. "It must be difficult having your sister here this year, and I wanted to make sure you're okay." His eyes were warm, and he smiled at me.

"Um, well, it's been . . . okay," I said, not sure what my response should be. Part of me didn't want to get into everything that had gone on, the other part was a teeny bit happy to have someone finally *ask* me how things were going, instead of just telling me what to do.

James nodded, encouraging me to continue.

"I mean, we're only in one class together, so it's fine," I said. Should I mention the fight? Or that Dezzie was upset about art? That didn't seem to be what he wanted to talk about, so I just stopped there.

"It can be difficult to have a sibling like yours to begin with," James said. "And then to have her come to *your* place . . . well, I bet it's been a tough start to the year. Are you okay with that?"

"Not really." The words slipped out before I could stop them. *Why* had I said that? Now he'd want to get into all the stuff that the counselor guy at SMARTS camp wanted to discuss—and I wasn't interested in any of it.

"I bet," he said. Then he was quiet for a minute, like he was waiting for me to say something. I didn't. "Do you want to tell me more about it?"

I shook my head.

"Look, Hamlet. This is a safe place. Nothing you say here can be repeated to anyone. Not your parents, your sister, or your friends—unless you want me to. So it's okay to tell me what you're thinking."

I understood what he meant, and I did trust him. It was hard not to, with his nice eyes and relaxed attitude. I could see why Ely came in here regularly. But suddenly I felt tired and empty. I was exhausted from the fight with Dezzie, stressed about English, worried about my ever-faltering pre-al class, and just sick of thinking about it all.

"I think I just want to go back to class."

James rubbed his beard and stared at the floor. When he looked up, he gave me a small smile. "That's cool. You don't have to talk today. But listen . . ." He rummaged through the pile of pamphlets on the coffee table and pulled out three or four small green cards. "These are what I call Go Cards," he said, and handed them to me. "When you want to talk, just write your name on a card and slip it under my office door. I'll send for you that same day."

I glanced down at them and then stuck them in my backpack. I didn't think I'd be using them, but I didn't want to be rude.

"Okay. Thanks." I struggled to get up from the chair. James unfolded from his and stood. He glanced at his watch.

"There's ten minutes left in this period, so you can go back to class." He scribbled on a late pass. "Thanks for coming in."

"Okay," I said. I took it and folded the corners down. "Thanks for checking on me."

He opened the door and I slipped out.

The hallway was empty, but given the way things had been going, if Shakespeare himself had been waiting there, I wouldn't have been surprised.

~ 11 ~

That afternoon I was supposed to meet Ty, Ely, and Judith at the Chilly Spoon to discuss the whole Dezzie/Saber/Mauri situation and probably argue more about my newly discovered Shakespearean curse. As I coasted into the tiny parking lot, I saw Ty's skateboard chained to the bike rack. He'd had one stolen two years before, and it was like he'd lost part of himself. He was determined not to lose this one to thieves. I parked my bike next to the board.

The Chilly Spoon is the best ice cream place in town. When you open the door, a whiff of homemade vanilla goodness wraps you in a desserty cloud. They make their own waffle cones and bowls all day, so the store has this warm, cozy smell. Ty and I had been coming here nearly weekly since they'd opened, and Ely and Judith joined us after we all started hanging out our first year at HoHo.

Ty was sitting at the rear table, the only one that didn't rock, back to me, alone. A tall white cup printed with the Spoon's logo sat on the pink and black checkered table-cloth. I plopped into the seat across from him.

"Hey," I said. "Where're Ely and Judith?"

He shrugged. "Ely said he'd be here after he walked Bunny, and I think Judith has a piano lesson." Ely's mom and dad got the family a dog after his sister had finished her cancer treatment, and had let her name him. Sometimes, when things at home went medieval to the extreme, I'd call Ely and ask him to meet me at the dog park. Iago would sit in the shade, lick his paws, and refuse to get dirty or interact with the other dogs, but Ely's dog was another story: Picture a seventy-five-pound chocolate Lab responding to "Bunny! Here boy!" when romping around, playing with the other people and their pets. It cracked me up every time.

"Of course Judith has piano." I rolled my eyes, but Ty knew that I was proud of her. Judith takes her music very seriously—she wants to be a singer/songwriter someday, and plays piano and guitar. Her voice is really good too.

I kicked at the rungs of my chair. "So what's up with the beverage? That better be water." I tried to sound like I was teasing, but I wasn't. Ty knew it too.

Whoever got to the Spoon first waited for the other before ordering. That way we could be sure to get complementary flavors. It was a bummer if you went in wanting orange sherbet and the other person already ordered mint chip—no sharing allowed, unless you're a fan of the ever-popular toothpaste/OJ combo.

He shrugged. "I wanted a frappe."

"Chocolate cherry?" I asked. It was one of his favorites.

"So what's up with Dezzie?" he continued, ignoring my question.

Something was off. Ty took our ice cream rule very seriously.

"Uh . . . everything okay?" I asked. I hadn't done anything wrong . . . had I?

"Yeah, totally." He brushed his bangs back and sipped at the straw, watching me the whole time. "So where'd you go during math?"

I told him about being sent to James's office, then Mrs. Wimple's not-so-subtle remarks after class. "I don't want to be Puck, and she knows it."

Ty rolled his eyes at me. "You'll be great. Don't worry about it." He chewed on his straw.

I waited a few seconds to see if he'd say anything else, but he didn't. Was his day as bad as mine? Giving up, I went to the counter and ordered two scoops of strawberry. It was a flavor that could go with nearly anything. If Ty wanted some, he could have a bite. I carried my cup to the table and sat, then tried to change the subject to get Ty talking.

"Something is definitely up with Saber and Mauri. They treat Dezzie like she's a pet. I'm surprised they haven't put a leash around her neck." A knot of irritation pulled tight in my middle. "It's even gotten worse since we got in that fight."

"What do you mean?" Ty slurped at the straw. A burbly sound came from the cup—he was almost finished.

"Dezzie doesn't want to talk to me, so she hangs out with them even more. She follows them around and talks Shakespeare all day. They're totally using her brains to pass English."

"Why do you care?" asked Ty. He rattled the empty container on the tabletop.

Honestly, I didn't know. I mean, cheating is wrong, so there was that part of it. They were taking advantage of her. But plenty of other kids cheated and it didn't bug me. I guess because she was my sister.

"Is there anything else going on?" Ty asked.

I swallowed a heaping spoonful of strawberry and immediately got brain freeze. I winced. "What do you mean, 'anything else'? I think this is enough to deal with, don't you?"

Ty's face pulled into a funny, tight expression: eyebrows scrunched, mouth in a thin line pulled down at the corners. "I don't know. What about KC and those guys? Aren't they around all the time?"

I shrugged and went for more ice cream. My spoon scraped against the paper bottom.

"I guess they're around," I said, when I'd swallowed again. "But they don't seem very interested in Dezzie. At least, not like Saber and Mauri."

Ty fiddled with his straw. "Maybe you're making a big deal over nothing. I mean, you guys are in a fight, right? Maybe that's making you more worried than you should be."

119

"Maybe, but I don't think so," I said.

"She's a smart kid," he said in an offhanded way. "She'll be fine."

But that was the problem—even though she's smart, Dezzie is still a kid. Ty wasn't going to be able to help with the situation—at least not while he was in this prickly mood—so I decided to let it go.

After a few minutes, Ely and Judith came in. Judith smiled and said hi, and when she thought I wasn't looking, I saw her glance from Ty to me and back to Ely with a raised eyebrow. *What* was going on?

"So what's up with English?" Ely asked. The way he attacked his bowl of chunky lumpy chocolate you'd think he was excavating an ancient burial ground—he ate around each white chocolate chunk, almond, and brownie bit.

"Dude, why do you eat it that way?" Judith asked. She gestured toward his bowl with her spoon. "You're dismantling that poor dessert."

"Saving the best parts for last," Ely muttered, all his concentration on separating the chocolate ice cream from a partially buried brownie cluster. He raised his eyes to me. "English. Spill."

I turned to Ty for help, but he was watching Felix, the best scooper at the Spoon, as he attempted to double stack blue bubblegum and what appeared to be cake batter for a little kid. The top flavor—cake batter or perhaps vanilla?—wobbled, but Felix smooshed it with his ice cream paddle and it held. Victory!

"Now Wimple wants me to play Puck." I paused.

"And you're surprised by this?" Judith asked. "I don't know why you can't just embrace it. Why so much with the hate-speare of the Bard?"

Her words reminded me of the practice session I'd held in my room. I had enjoyed reading the words, but I just couldn't get into this whole idea. Keeping my eyes on Felix, I didn't say anything. The kid turned away from the counter, a just-in-case cup under his cone.

"Double your creativity points for that one." Ely clacked his spoon with Judith's, acknowledging her joke.

"Seriously. I don't get what the big deal is," Ty said, attention back to us. "It's just the Bard, Ham. Think of him as your unlovable uncle, and saying the words won't be a big deal."

How could I explain that that was what I was afraid of? That making my "talent" public was like I was embracing the whole Shakespeare thing—crazy uncle and all. Of anyone, you'd think Ty would be able to get it. He knew my family the best. I tried again.

"It's extreme Shakespeare," I said. "Too much . . . just like my family. And that's not me."

"You're right," Ely said. We turned to him. Ice cream gone, all that remained in his cup were lumps of filling. They looked kind of gross out of their creamy context.

He crunched a mouthful of leftovers. "But you're not extreme anything. So no one is going to think that."

"Exactly," Judith said. "It's not like we're all of a sudden going to change what we think of you because of a stupid English project. You're overstressing about this."

"I might change what I think," Ely said. Ty threw a balled-up napkin at him. Ely ducked in mock horror.

"Would it be the most terrible thing in the world if you love it?" Judith asked. "I think my recitals are fun. Being in front of an audience rocks. It gives you energy."

I appreciated the pep talk, but it didn't help. The feeling that I had in James's office, of being done with it all, came back. I slid out of my seat and stood up.

"Leaving?" Judith asked.

"I'm going to get some to take home."

Ty crumpled his cup and walked to the counter with me.

"Are you *sure* you're okay?" I asked him again. "Because it really seems like something's bugging you."

He waited a minute. "I'm fine. Seriously. It's just been an off day."

It was a lame response, but I knew not to push him. Felix asked what I wanted, and I ordered some berry crunch to go.

"That's Dezzie's favorite flavor," Ty said, seeming happy to change the subject. "I thought you were barely speaking."

"Yeah, but Mom's tried three new seventeenth-century recipes this week," I joked, remembering the artichoke pie, orange pudding, and something called "pickled broom buds." Fight or no fight, my sister needed something from this century. And maybe it would hold her attention long enough for me to point out what her not-friends really wanted from her. It was worth a shot.

I got my ice cream and said my good-byes. Ely and Judith paused in conversation about their Globe Theatre—seems that they couldn't get their second level right—and Judith followed me out to my bike.

"There's something you need to know," she said.

"Okay, what?" I was busy tucking Dezzie's ice cream into the basket.

"Someone likes you," she said, using her very serious voice. Squeals and squees are for telling people they are liked, not serious voices. I glanced up at her.

"Someone who?" I tried to keep my tone neutral. Did she know who was responsible for the locker pigs?

She licked her lips and nodded her head toward the door. "Ty," she said.

At the same time as a bowling ball settled into my stomach, a lightbulb went on over my head. It explained why he'd been acting so strange, but . . .

"He doesn't know origami."

Judith's face was one big question mark. I reminded her about the swine collection in my locker, and she laughed.

"It's not funny!"

"It kind of is," Judith responded, then tried to smooth things over. "But if it's not Ty, then who is it?"

"I have no idea. I'm hoping it's Carter Teegan," I said shyly.

"You think *Carter* knows origami?" Judith's skepticism was hard to miss. "He barely *opens* his notebooks in class, let alone folds the paper in them."

"Whatever." I never should have said anything about Carter. This conversation needed to end. Pronto. "Anyway, Ty doesn't like me, like me. He may as well be my brother."

"My word," Judith said, and raised her hand in a mock Boy Scout salute. "Sorry, but true."

"How do you know?" I said.

"He told me." She tinkered with the paper bag. "He's been freaking out about it."

I could see why. I swung a leg over my bike seat, ready to leave this behind.

"Look, I didn't want to tell you. I knew it'd creep you out, but I thought you should know."

"Gee, *thanks*." That came out sharper than I intended. "Look, I need to think about this, okay?" I needed to leave. Fast.

She nodded. "Sure."

Before she could say anything else, I was gone. And . . . *scene.*

ꙮ iii ꙮ

Hey, Dezzie," I called, "I brought you some berry crunch!" I tossed the paper bag onto the kitchen island. Hopefully she wouldn't mind that it was a bit melted. I'd taken the long way home so I could think about what Judith said. And, no surprise: I didn't know what to do and I wanted to forget I ever heard the conversation in the first place.

"Huzzah!" she cheered, skittering out of the den and launching herself into the kitchen. Ice cream was one of the only things that could make Dezzie act her age. I brought some back whenever I could, because I loved her reaction. Since Mom and Dad shopped at a local organic farm to get the ingredients for their Renaissance-era meals, ice cream rarely appeared in our house (although lots of giant cuts of meat and bushels of veggies did).

I didn't always tell them about my Chilly Spoon trips because I went much more often than Mom would like. She's not into sweets. Dad's more relaxed, but even so, he feels that ice cream should be for special occasions, while I believe it's a way of life.

Dad popped his head around the doorframe. "Didn't happen to bring home a chocolate frappe, did you?" His eyes were hopeful behind his oval reading glasses. He's a sucker for the occasional contemporary treat. I shook my head.

"Sorry."

"I need to find this week's lecture notes for Birth of the Sonnet. Your mother will be home shortly—she's at her Shakespeare on the Common planning meeting."

While he spoke, Dezzie attacked the cup like it was an immersion project. A dribble of pink slipped from the corner of her mouth. I handed her a napkin.

Dad disappeared in the direction of his office.

I leaned against the counter, watching my sister scrape every last drop of her dessert from the paper container. Sitting on a counter stool, wearing that white T-shirt with the embroidered ring of flowers at the hem and on one sleeve, spoon clenched in her right fist, staring into the cup, eyebrows drawn together in concentration, she could have been anyone's little sister—anyone's *normal* little sister. And then she had to speak.

"Did you know," she said, dropping the spoon into the empty cup, "that precursors to ice cream were available in ancient Persian societies? And that even the Roman Empire would serve flavored snow after banquets?"

I shook my head, irritated by the quiz. "Nope."

"The first recorded recipe for true ice cream was printed in 1718, in a book called *Mrs. Mary Eales's Receipts*. And . . ."

"And I'm not interested in learning any more," I said, patience gone. "You could thank me instead."

She froze. "Oh, sorry. I just . . ." She faltered, glancing around the kitchen as though an escape hatch would make itself visible.

"It's fine." I paused. "Look, I know things between us have been different lately," I began, trying to figure out a way to approach the Mauri/Saber subject.

"If by 'different' you mean that you made some unconscionable comments to me, then I agree," Dezzie said.

I wasn't sure what "unconscionable" meant, but I got the gist of what she was saying.

"You insulted me first," I pointed out.

"I made an accidental slip of the tongue," she said, crushing the paper cup. "*You* were malicious." She scowled. "I wouldn't be malicious."

I wanted to point out that her giggle at Saber's art class "bacon fingers" comment when I dropped my brushes was pretty malicious, but that would lead to more arguing.

"Okay, you're right—as always. I'm sorry." I rushed through the apology. Then it occurred to me: Maybe if I first let Dezzie do what she was good at—solving puzzles—she'd be more receptive to the idea that Saber and Mauri weren't what they seemed.

"Do you think you could help me with something?" I asked. I didn't want to bring it up, but it was the only chance I had at getting her to listen to me.

"I will try my best to do so," she responded. "What is the nature of your query?"

I told her the story of the origami pigs and the first-day note. I left out the part about Ty liking me—I couldn't bring myself to say those words out loud or hear what Dezzie's opinion of that situation was. As I spoke, she folded her hands and rested them on top of the island. She was a mini psychiatrist. All she needed were some glasses and a notebook to complete the look.

"It is an obvious ploy to get your attention, Hamlet," she said. "Preadolescent male peacocking behavior."

"Peacocking?" What was she talking about?

"Males of any species show off to garner female attention. Someone is designing the origami to get you to notice him."

"But I don't know who is leaving them there," I huffed. "If it's a ploy to get my attention, I don't know who I should be directing my attention *at*!" Frustration built in me. Why had I thought this was the way to go?

"If you are more observant, I am sure you will find that someone is putting on a display for you. That is the person unobtrusively visiting your locker," she finished, satisfied with her solution. "Also, I should be interested in seeing the craftsmanship of the animals, if you are inclined to share them with me. The art of paper folding requires patience and precision."

I didn't know what she meant by "display," and I didn't

want to ask any more questions. Patience and precision were what I needed to steer this conversation back to Saber and Mauri—my original target.

"I'll let you know if I notice any strutting birds in the hallway." Not the lead-in I was hoping for, but I barreled on to the real point of this conversation. (And, really, "displays"?!?) "Also, there's something you might need to know."

Dezzie raised an eyebrow at me. "What?"

"It's about Saber and Mauri. They aren't your real friends. They are just—"

"How would you know?" Dezzie snapped, surprising me. Oof! Smooth Transition Failure.

"You don't like them. It is obvious that you are envious of their social stature and, thus, my interaction with them. They've never invited you to sit at their lunch table, I'd wager." She folded her arms and smirked, all friendly confidante behavior gone. Seeing such a mean-middle-school expression on her second-grade face disoriented me.

How did she have everything so wrong?

"That's *not* it," I said, irritated by her tone and newfound attitude—and unable to believe that Saber and Mauri were causing the second fight I'd ever had with my sister. "I don't want to sit at their lunch table, nor do I want to hang out with their group of friends. I'm trying to help you see what they really want from you."

Dezzie tossed her crushed cup and spoon into our

recycling bin. "I don't need your help anymore, Hamlet. I am doing just fine on my own." She turned her back to me and left.

Seething with anger, I called after her, "I think 'peacocking' is a lame explanation! Boys aren't as immersed in ornithology as you are!"

When she didn't respond, I made one more jab—"And forget getting any more ice cream from *me*!"—and stomped up to my bedroom.

Fight total: two.

And that was two fights more than my sister and I had ever had.

~ iV ~

T he Monday after the ice cream fight, I struggled through the pre-al test and found that
my herd of pigs went up to six. I added the
latest one—made from floral origami paper—to the others
on my locker shelf, then went to lunch.

For the first few minutes of the period, my thoughts
stayed firmly in my locker. I hadn't noticed any "peacocking" around me this morning. Even though Dezzie's
theory didn't make too much sense to me, it was all I had
to go on. I tossed possibilities around in my brain, ruling
anyone else out to force Carter into being the culprit. I
was about to imagine his confession when Judith gave me
a funny look.

"Isn't that your sister?" she asked. I spun around in my
seat.

Sure enough, across the caf, I saw Dezzie's mess of
dark curls sitting substantially lower in her chair than
Saber's and Mauri's ponytails. She was sucking on a juice-
box straw acting like she sat there every day. My heart was
replaced with a cold lead weight.

"What's she doing there?" Ely said.

"Saber and Mauri asked her to stay for lunch in art a few days ago." I shrugged, acting like it was no big deal. "I guess Mom said it was okay." I plopped my sandwich onto the table. What was it about eighth grade that caused me to lose my appetite so often? I could only imagine what was in store for me in high school.

"Dude, no offense, Ham," Judith said, "but why would *they* want Dezzie to sit with them?"

"None taken." I paused. "They're using Dezzie to get ahead in English," I explained. "She's feeding them answers to our homework and she doesn't even know it." In spite of our most recent argument, the idea still disgusted me. I didn't want to turn and stare at them, but I had to know what was going on at the table. Judith and Ely gave me the play-by-play.

"I think they're asking her a lot of questions," Ely said.

"Yup," Judith agreed. "And Mauri has a notebook that she keeps writing in."

"Rip-off jerks," Ty muttered. He took a bite from his sandwich. I wasn't meeting his eyes. The info from Judith was too new; around him, I felt like my skin contained a bag of jangly triangles. But his assessment of the Dezzie situation was right on.

"What else are they doing?"

"Laughing," Judith said.

"Is it a good laugh?" It was so frustrating not to be able to see them.

"What?" Ely cried. "They're *laughing*. What's a 'good' laugh?"

Judith rolled her eyes at him. "Of *course* you can't tell the difference—you're about as observant as a wind-up toy. Good thing *you're* not on this side of the table too, or Ham would have no idea what's going on." She directed that last part at Ty, who threw a potato chip at her.

"Excuse me," I said. "In need of information over here."

"It's not a friend laugh," Judith evaluated, "more like an 'isn't it cute' laugh. They keep looking at each other over Dezzie's head when she's done talking. Or maybe it's more like an 'are you impressed too' laugh. Hard to say."

They were making fun of her, I knew it. But I couldn't prove it. And Dezzie didn't seem to realize—or she didn't care, which was a possibility. We hadn't spoken in a few days, and silence was becoming routine in the Kennedy household. But despite our argument, I still felt as though she was my responsibility while she was at HoHo.

Without saying a word to anyone, I slipped out of my chair and crossed the caf. A few seconds later I was standing behind Dezzie. I tapped her on the shoulder. Mauri, next to her, slid a notebook off the table and out of sight. Like I didn't know what *that* was for. Whatever.

"Hey, it's Omelette," KC said. When I glared at him, he gave me a wide, innocent smile.

"Ha-ha," I said, channeling Ely's dry sarcasm.

"Oh, I cracked you up!" KC laughed. "Get it? Cracked? Eggs? Omelette?"

I turned my back on him.

"Hi Hamlet," Dezzie said, tilting her head up to me. "How is your lunch?" Her words were forced.

"Fine," I said, trying to ignore the curious expressions on Saber's, Mauri's, and the boys' faces. Of course Carter was there too, which made it harder for me to concentrate. He ran his hands through his hair, making it spike up in all directions. Why did he have to be so cute? He was munching on what appeared to be a roast beef and pickle sandwich. He let out a loud burp, and the boys laughed.

Oh, ew.

"Wanna sit down?" Saber asked, acting her part as queen of the table.

"I'm good. But I thought you might want to come over and see Ty and Ely before the end of lunch," I directed to Dezzie. I hadn't planned what I was going to say, and the lame words came out of my mouth in a weak trickle.

"Why?" she said, sounding genuinely puzzled. It was as if I was asking her to do something she'd never thought of—like bungee jumping from HoHo's roof. In Dezzie's world, I knew she said it because, logically, there was no reason for her to come over to our table—she sees Ty and Ely fairly often and had nothing new to say to them. That's not how it went over, though. Everyone cracked up like it was the funniest thing they'd ever heard. KC snorted milk from his nose, but I think he was practicing to do that on purpose.

I fought rising anger and annoyance. "Because they want to see you," I answered through gritted teeth. Dezzie, for her part, had realized the group's misinterpretation of her word. A flicker of concern crossed her face, but the laughter brightened her back up again.

"Tell them I'll see them later," she said, tossing her hair. "I'll come say hi just before the bell. I don't want to miss any *displays* going on at this table." That last part was said with a knowing glance at the boys.

What? Did she think Carter's burp-fest was a display? Maybe I was right!

"Yeah," Mauri said, forcing my train of thought to stop at idiot station. "Why would you want to hang out with them? I mean, they *are* probably talking about nerdalicious stuff like their reading and projects, but whatever." Mauri flipped her hair to another round of laughs. I took deep breaths through my nose, trying not to make things worse by opening my mouth.

Dezzie nodded. "True, but that's what you've been talking about this whole time. And you're not nerdalicious," she added helpfully.

Mauri's face turned as pink as her new nail polish shade. "Whatever," she snapped. "Go hang out with your sister if that's what you really want to do."

"Yeah," echoed Saber. "I'm sure her friends are *way* more fun than we are. Maybe they're talking about the Ren Faire or something." She gave me a meaningful look. I wanted to give her a meaningful look too, if you get me.

The girls turned to each other over my sister's head, pretending that Dezzie wasn't there, and started a conversation about shopping over the weekend. And about how *some*one would have been able to go on the next one if *she* hadn't suddenly disappeared from the lunch table.

I'd seen it happen before. The two of them were champion ignorers. In two seconds, you could go from being part of their world to just a satellite in orbit. I knew enough not to be interested in being friends with them in the first place, so it had never happened to me, but I'd watched the damage they inflicted on other girls—and now were inflicting on my sister. Dezzie's eyes narrowed—whether at me or at them, I couldn't tell.

"Get thee to a nunnery, Hamlet," she said.

"What?" I gasped, shocked that a.) she would dismiss me from the lunch table, and b.) that she was using the phrase Mom employed when I was sent to my room for "being impudent."

"*What* did you just say?"

136

"Did you hear something?" Mauri asked. A smile danced at the edge of her lips.

"I think there's a bug in here," said Saber. She was also trying not to laugh.

"Must I translate? If you prefer: *Get lost.* I'm staying here." Dezzie turned square to the table and I was faced with the back of her head—and a whole lot of anger.

I bent down so that my mouth was just behind her ear. "You curly-haired *wretch*," I hissed, throwing another Shakespeare Slam her way. "I am *totally* going to get you for this." I stalked back to my table.

"How'd it go?" Ty asked, full of concern. "Are you okay?" He reached over to pat my arm or back—something he'd done countless times before, but this time it felt different. Was Judith right? I dodged him, speechless, and scooted my chair farther away from his.

"It tanked, yo. Obviously," Ely answered for me. His dreads bobbed like ocean buoys. "What were you hoping to do? Get her to come back here with you?"

I coughed and got my vocal cords to work again. "Yeah. Stupid idea, I know." The bell rang and I stuffed my nearly whole lunch into my bag. I didn't look at Ty.

"What were they talking about?" Judith asked as we made our way through the crowd to our next class.

"More English assignments, of course," I said. "And some shopping trip they went on this weekend. They even hinted that they want Dezzie to go next time."

"Can't imagine your sister being interested in shopping," she replied. I shrugged. For all I knew, she could be planning an immersion project on teenage shopping mall habits and the use of sparkly accessories to deliniate social status. We were standing outside of Judith's French class.

"So," she said, "have you said anything to Ty yet?"

I was hoping she'd forgotten. "Umm . . . no," I said. "Not exactly."

"You need to talk to him soon, Ham," she said, "or things are going to get strange between the two of you."

"Like they aren't already?" I asked, mentally reliving the dodged hand-pat. What if he wanted to kiss me? How was I supposed to deal with *that*?

Eeeeek! That hadn't occurred to me before.

My best friend probably wanted to kiss me, and that prospect was about as appealing as Mom's cooking.

❦ V ❧

"I do not understand why you are so upset with me, Hamlet," Dezzie said that night. I'd come home from school and apologized again. Even though I felt like I didn't need to, I was sick of the silence and awkwardness with my sister. Too much awkwardness in my life these days. We were sitting on her bed, trying to work out what had happened at lunch, Iago snoozing between us. "I'm only doing what you told me to do on the first day of school: blend in. And it's working."

How to explain to a genius that sometimes you need more than brains to navigate junior high? I took a deep breath.

"Because, Dezzie, you can't just insult me in front of them! Then it looks like we're not on the same team."

"But you don't *want* to be on their team," she pointed out to me for the fifth or sixth time, in a maddeningly patient tone. "You don't want to be friends with them. They are friends with me."

"But that's just it," I said for what felt like the zillionth time. "They. Are. Not. Your. Friends." I whomped her pillow on the bedspread to emphasize each word. Iago sprang off the mattress, glared at me, and trotted to the door to be let out.

"Then why would they invite me to go shopping with them this weekend?" Dezzie said, closing the door behind him. She smoothed the wrinkles both he and the pillow had left on the bed.

"Because they want you to help them more!" I groaned and flopped over. "Why don't you get it?"

"And why do *you* always have to think poorly of them?"

"Because they're mean and sneaky."

She didn't understand.

"I'm not discussing this anymore," she said. "You may stay if you want to preview our next unit in art class, though." She pulled a giant stack of books that she'd borrowed from Ms. Finch-Bean off her dresser.

"Fine." Maybe I'd get another chance to convince her that Saber and Mauri were up to no good. She cracked a surrealists book open. There were lots of paintings of clocks melting, people with distorted bodies and really long legs, and flies.

"Ick," I said, and slid the book away. "This stuff creeps me out. I like the abstract stuff we're doing in class so much better."

"I find the surrealists fascinating," Dezzie responded. "I am very much looking forward to concluding our Jackson

Pollock unit and moving on to these artists who use their imagination to stretch the boundaries of reality."

"I like my reality just they way it is—with no flies in it. So what do they want to know about the play?" I'd try another tactic. There was no way I was going to let this go. Because if I stopped focusing on Dezzie, I'd have to deal with the pig situation. Or English. And neither option was a good one.

"Elemental things—why the characters are doing what they're doing, what Shakespeare's language means, what some of the themes are . . ."

"That's a lot of the stuff we talk about in class. See? They're using you."

"Maybe they don't comprehend it in class." Dezzie shrugged and closed the art book. "I need to work on my calculus equations, okay?" She slipped off the bed and went over to her desk. This was my cue.

"Are they nice to you?" I straightened her covers again.

"Of course," she replied. "Do you think I'd talk to people who openly made fun of me?"

It was the not-so-openly stuff I was concerned about. And the fact that the people who were so nice to her weren't so nice to me—it wasn't like Saber and Mauri to be accepting of Kennedy-esque differences.

"You don't ever wonder why they want you to hang out with them so much?" I asked from the doorway, making a last-ditch effort.

"I'd rather not," said Dezzie. "It's the first time I've had school friends. Can we not talk about this anymore?"

Her response sank my heart and my desire to prod her any more. Of course it was the first time she'd had friends in school—or been in school, for that matter—and why should I care if Saber and Mauri wanted to know all about Shakespeare from the little genius? She could help them. And anyway, I was going to need her help in pre-al as soon as that test grade came back too. There was no way I'd gotten higher than a D—I hadn't understood a single question. Of course, if I'd paid better attention, maybe I would have.

If she was helping them and they were nice to her, what did it have to do with me? Even if Saber and Mauri weren't the kind of people I'd hang out with, that didn't necessarily make them wrong for Dezzie, right?

Right?

"Wrong," said Mr. Symphony in class the next day. He smacked our tests on his desk. Everyone jumped. "Wrong, wrong, wrong. Only two of you received grades higher than a seventy." He peered at us over the top of his glasses.

At least I wasn't alone in my failure.

"This is the worst performance by a pre-algebra class that I've seen in twenty years of teaching," he said. His face was growing darker and darker purple, like an eggplant. "Is anyone paying attention in class? Are you making an effort to follow along? Because it doesn't seem like it."

We shot guilty looks at one another. No one spoke. Mr. S. wasn't really expecting us to answer anyway. He was off on a rant. He put the tests down and rubbed his eyes.

"You need to be up to speed before you take exams in December," he explained in a softer voice. "Those are the qualifiers for your math track in high school. Your final grades just reinforce your placement. So everyone needs to do their best from the very beginning."

I tuned him out. I already knew I'd bombed the test. And, okay, it was partially as a result of not paying attention in class, but really—why does math have letters in it? Letters + Numbers, like Me + Ty = Two things that should never get together.

"And so, many of you will be attending TLC sessions between now and the next test," Mr. Symphony finished.

What had I missed now?

"If you received a note from me on your exam, you are one of the students involved in the first round of the pilot program. We'll begin class as a group, then the TLC students will leave, work with their tutors, and I'll have a smaller group in class. At the end of four weeks, we'll switch." He stifled the groans and complaints with a frown, and passed the tests back.

It was just what I'd expected—a big fat 57 circled in red at the top of the page, a "See me—TLC 1" scrawled underneath it.

For the remainder of the class, I tried to pay attention and take detailed notes on what Mr. S. was saying. By the end of the period, I had a slightly better understanding of x and y, but only slightly. As much as it didn't appeal to me, going to TLC would probably save my mathematical future.

When the bell rang, it was easy to see who else had failed as badly as me. Ely and Ty gave me hopeful looks, then left. They were the two who'd passed. Perhaps *they* were actually related to Dezzie.

KC *was* in the group. He plopped his notebook on his head and whispered "osmosis" to me. A giggle escaped me, against my will. At least there would be entertainment in TLC. It was like he was constantly onstage—the spotlight was always on him. Too bad he'd be doing sets in our big production.

"So the prince can't do algebra either?" he teased. That remark dried up my humor. He'd make a better Puck than me, I thought. Carter, also in our bunch of the pre-al challenged, rolled his eyes. My heart thumped.

There were four or five other kids who would be going to TLC. We bunched around Mr. Symphony's desk. I didn't speak or look at anyone else. There was no shame in needing extra help, I knew that, but being forced into a group for tutoring *was* embarrassing. Especially when Carter needed it too.

"Now then," Mr. S. said, "I'll keep this brief, as I have another class due. You are all here because, even though your grades on your tests weren't above passing, the papers showed promise. This means I think you can catch up before the next exam. You'll go to TLC beginning tomorrow."

We grunted and shuffled our feet. No one wanted to ask a question, even though I'm sure everyone had as many as me—what did he mean by "showed promise"? If we were being sent away because we could catch up, what did that mean about the rest of the class? But I'm sure the other thing that I was thinking of wasn't on anyone else's mind—how could I have a newly discovered brilliance in English, but not even break a sixty on a math test?

Mr. S. dismissed us. I caught Carter's eye on the way out the door. He offered me an encouraging smile. Or was it directed at Chrissy Li, behind me? Hard to tell. I nearly melted in my shoes. Maybe being in TLC with him wouldn't be so bad after all. We could be study partners. Away from Saber and Mauri, I might actually be able to talk to him (although, if my pounding heart and sweaty hands were any indication, I'd probably just squeak stupidly).

I took a deep breath, determined to get this over with and approach him.

"Hi Hamlet," chirped a voice at my elbow. "See any peacocks today?" I nearly tripped.

"Hey, you scared me." I smiled down at Dezzie, thoughts of Carter blocking any lingering frustration from the previous night's talk in her bedroom. "What are you doing all the way over here?"

She held up a pile of papers. "I'm bringing tutoring sign-up forms to Mr. Symphony. He is sending several students in for extra help."

"Guess so," I said through suddenly dry lips.

"He needs to fill them out and I'll bring them back, and then go meet Mom," she said, taking another step. I hadn't noticed that we'd stopped walking.

"Uh, sure." I moved in a random direction, not thinking about where I needed to go. I was hit by a realization tsunami.

Dezzie spent this class period in TLC each day. Half of my math class would be in there with her. Including me. Add that to her track record of telling my parents everything that went on in the halls of HoHo . . .

My appetite might never come back.

After dinner that night, I tried to get Dezzie to help me with pre-al. My hope was that between her tutoring and begging Mr. Symphony not to send me for extra help, I'd be able to catch up enough to avoid this round of TLC. She was busy with calculus, though, and was determined to do some extra reading on the surrealists before bedtime. Although carrying the brains of a retired rocket scientist, she still needed the same amount of sleep as a regular seven-year-old, so she usually went to bed before me.

"If you're coming in to TLC, I don't see why you need

me to work with you now," she said, tapping her pencil against her math book. Iago was curled up on her bed, which lately had been meeting his "freshness standards" more than mine.

"I don't want to come in for the help," I explained. "It was just one bad test." Sitting in TLC and being tutored with kids in my grade—while my seven-year-old sister watched—made my stomach pucker tighter than my mother's drawstring purse.

"Well, I can't do it now," Dezzie said. This was the third time I'd asked, and she was getting irritable. "You'll just have to wait until tomorrow, like everyone else."

"Fine." I closed her door harder than necessary on my way out.

I reopened it, causing the dog to jump. He hopped off the bed and left the room, rolling his eyes at me as he passed. Disturbing him twice in two nights? He'd be on his way to find some of my shoes to chew, I was sure.

"Look, don't tell Mom and Dad—even by accident," I said. "I really don't want them to know about this."

"I won't," she replied, eyes on her book, back to me.

"Seriously, Dezzie. Promise."

"I *won't*," she said again. "I have to do my work. Don't you have some lines to practice or something?"

Grrr. I closed the door again.

In my own room, I spread the math book, test papers, and homework assignment across the bed and stared at them for a half hour. Dezzie was right. There was no way I'd be able to learn pre-algebra on my own in one night to the point where I wouldn't need to go to TLC the next day. The attempt would be as useless as trying to wear the shredded sneaker I caught sight of, sticking out from under my bed.

The other thing Dezzie was right about? I had lines to review. I opened my copy of *Midsummer* to the first act, where Puck has been instructed to put fairy dust in the eyes of Demetrius, but he gets confused and puts the love potion on Lysander's instead. I whispered the words out loud, afraid Mom or Dad would hear me and ask way more questions than I had answers for.

"Pretty soul! she durst not lie/Near this lack-love, this kill-courtesy./Churl, upon thy eyes I throw/All the power this charm doth owe." The words slid like satin from my mouth. I didn't know what "churl" meant, exactly, but I knew it wasn't a compliment.

Shakespeare had it right, I thought. If fairies were the ones messing with me—putting pigs in my locker and making my best friend want more than friendship—perhaps, like in the play, their king would order everything to go back to normal at the end.

I tossed the book aside and flopped onto my pillows, relishing the notion of a world where I wouldn't have to do anything except worry about math.

~Vi~

hen I arrived in art the next day, Saber, Mauri, and Dezzie were in their usual spots at the table, already talking.

"I had the best dream last night," Mauri chirped.

Dezzie, jotting stuff in her notebook, forehead creased (like any seven-year-old, she still has trouble holding a pen or pencil for too long), put her pencil down and gave Mauri a patient smile—but not before I saw annoyance flash across her face.

"What was it about?" she asked.

"I got this new cell phone—it was pink and sparkly—and anyone I wanted to call would just, like, pop out of it when I called them. I didn't even have to dial their number, just say their name and they'd be there."

"Cool," Saber said, at the same time Dezzie asked, "You dream about magic cell phones?"

Saber dropped her pencil and quizzed Mauri on who she tried to call. Then the two of them speculated about who they would call if they had a *real* cell phone that did that.

"Theo Christmas, definitely," Mauri said.

"And Parker McKenzie," Saber responded. They giggled.

"Who would *you* call, Dezzie?" They asked the question at nearly the same time. It was as though they'd planned it.

"Stephen Hawking, of course," she said, without thinking. He's a physicist whose work she really admires. Saber and Mauri wore identical confused expressions. Clearly, they were expecting another musician or actor.

"Who's *he?*" Saber asked, before Dezzie could add more mathematicians or scientists to her list.

"He's, ummm . . ." She bit her lip and glanced at me for help.

"This really cool punk singer," I said. They looked like they weren't buying it. "From the seventies. Dezzie's into old music." Dezzie nodded her head.

"I'm surprised you haven't heard of him," she said with an airy tone to her voice.

Saber and Mauri shifted on their stools, clearly uncomfortable.

"I think my cousin likes him," Mauri said. "His name sounds familiar." Saber was quick to agree.

I dropped my pencil on the floor so they wouldn't see me stifling a laugh. I didn't know why Dezzie wouldn't tell the truth about who Hawking was—he had discovered that some particles can escape black holes, which was pretty cool, but it was way better to see Saber and Mauri pretending like they knew he was a singer all along. I went to the sink to wash my hands before the late bell.

When I returned, the conversation had taken a turn.

"So you really like the scene when Hermia tells Demetrius to follow her into the wood, so he can see Lysander and Helena escape," Saber said as I approached.

"It epitomizes the themes of the play," Dezzie said. "Hamlet. We were just—"

"What do you think we'll be covering next?" Mauri asked, cutting Dezzie off. Like I didn't know what they were up to. Ms. Finch-Bean collected our expressionist paintings and we were set to begin a new unit.

"Surrealism," both Dezzie and Ms. Finch-Bean said at the same time. The bell rang.

For the rest of class, we watched slides of those same melting clocks and distorted people that I'd been looking at with Dezzie. Lots of kids thought they were cool, especially the boys.

"That Salvador guy must have been on a lot of drugs to paint that," Nirmal Grover said. The image was of three ladies with no arms, with these shadowy figures and unconnected images around them. And, of course, flies. Lots of flies. If you looked hard enough, you were supposed to be able to see a bullfighter. Thanks to the creepy bugs, I wasn't looking hard at all.

"Actually, Dalí was famous for *not* drinking alcohol or

using drugs of any kind," Ms. Finch-Bean replied. "As a matter of fact, he once said, 'I don't do drugs, I am drugs.'"

"Then some drugs might have made him normal," KC said. Everyone laughed.

By the time class ended, I'd had my fill of flies and Dalí's strange world—which, come to think of it, seemed more and more like my own: completely surreal. However, I'd have happily stayed for two more periods if it meant avoiding my trip to TLC later that morning.

"See you soon," I said to Dezzie as we were leaving. Saber and Mauri shot glances at each other. Uh-oh.

"Staying for lunch again, Dezzie?" Saber asked. Her face was a mask of innocence.

"No. I have other work to do this afternoon." We'd stopped in the middle of the hall. Kids streamed around us, trying to get to their next classes. I frantically tried to come up with something to distract them and save the situation, but my mind, like on a pre-al test, was a big fat blank.

"So when will you see Hamlet?" This time it was Mauri who did the asking. "Maybe next period?" She said that last part with a sly smile.

"We're going to be late," I said as the warning bell buzzed. Although I made a point of her not telling our parents, I'd forgotten to tell Dezzie not to mention me going to TLC to Saber or Mauri.

Saber looked nervous. "We can't be late for history again," she muttered to Mauri. "Let's go."

"See you later," Mauri called as Saber tugged her down the hall. I was also going to be late to English if I didn't hurry, but . . .

"Did you tell them anything?" I stopped walking and put my hands on my hips.

Dezzie shifted from side to side. "In our previous class, Saber and Mauri inquired after my pursuits during my Learning Center period. I informed them that I typically read and speak with the parent volunteers, but that today some students were coming in for math help and I'd welcome the change."

"And you didn't mention that I would be there?"

Dezzie shook her head. "Although I believe they inferred that based upon your comment."

Great. This was my own fault—of course. Frustration swept through me.

I muttered good-bye, left her in the hall, and jogged to Mrs. Wimple's class, thumping into my seat just as the bell rang.

"Ms. Kennedy, I'd like you to read the part of Pyramus," Mrs. Wimple said from the front of the room. Although listening to the excruciating stumbles of my classmates was torture, it was much better than the caged animal feeling that came over me whenever she spoke the words I dreaded.

"Uh," I started, trying to stall. "I thought I was Puck?" And he wasn't in this scene.

"During class time you have the opportunity to read a variety of roles," she said crisply.

"And Mr. Spencer will read Thisbe," she said, moving on to the next in line for the scene. Obviously, she thought that ignoring my protests would be the only way this would happen. Ty groaned.

At least we were nearing the end of the play. Bottom and the other players were performing for the couples before the wedding ceremony. I skimmed the pages as Mrs. Wimple assigned the other readers.

When I realized what lines we'd be reading, I wanted to dive under my desk. Pyramus and Thisbe were "lovers." Lovers separated by a wall. The irony—that "love" (or something like it; something that made me want to yurk) was building a wall through the friendship Ty and I shared—didn't escape me. Ha-ha. Thanks, Shakespeare, I thought bitterly.

Nirmal, reading Theseus, began. I barely listened to his lines. I was concentrating so hard on looking at the page in front of me that he could have been reciting nursery rhymes instead of Shakespeare and I wouldn't have noticed. My heart thudded in my chest and my head buzzed.

My turn. And I'd make sure Mrs. Wimple didn't assign me any more parts.

I kept my eyes on the book and slid a finger under each word as I read it.

"O . . . grim . . . looked . . ." The forced slowness made me hyper-aware of everyone in the class listening, and I was sure Mrs. Wimple was staring at me the whole time.

When I finished that first line, my hands were sweating.

A few sections later Ty came in, saying, "My love thou art, my love I think."

My mouth went dry. Think again, Ty. I muttered back, "Think what thou wilt, I am thy lover's grace."

A few lines later, it got even worse:

"O, kiss me through the hole of this vile wall!" I nearly choked on the line, but refused to look up from my book.

Ty, across the aisle from me, decided to ham it up. He leaned *waay* out from his desk, toward me, for his next line. Then he whispered: "I kiss the wall's hole, not your lips at all." And he laid a big air-smooch near my face.

My stomach churned and burned. My hands, neck, and hairline were all damp, my shirt stuck to my back in a gross patch. But I never once looked up. I wasn't "acting," "enunciating," or doing anything else that Mrs. Wimple had accused me of before. And I certainly wasn't going all goo-goo likey-likey on Ty through my character.

We finished the scene with ten minutes left in the period. Mrs. Wimple closed her book. A bunch of kids sighed, probably grateful that it was over. I know I was.

"You should be working on those theaters," Mrs. Wimple said. "Mr. Hoffstedder is going to be expecting a progress report on them from you tomorrow."

Ugh. Ty and I still needed to finish the upper level on ours.

Mrs. Wimple stood by my desk, preventing me from leaving. "That performance was quite different from the last one," she said, staring straight at me. I studied the zipper on my backpack.

"Well, I didn't practice this time," I mumbled, hoping that she'd accept that the last few times had been an accident or something. She narrowed her eyes like she was trying to X-ray my brain.

"I don't believe you," she said. Without meaning to, I gasped. She certainly wasn't making any effort to hide her feelings, was she?

Even though I'd asked for it, her words stung.

In pre-al, Mr. S. collected our homework and gave us the day's assignments after taking attendance. My assignments so far today: one period of embarrassment in English, followed by teacher torment and pre-al.

"Now then," he began, "those of you who are launching our pilot program may leave. I expect you to go straight to The Learning Center, where you will finish the remainder of the class period."

No one moved. My face burned as hot as a charcoal grill and my legs felt as though they'd been replaced by iron bowling balls. How was I going to get up?

"Do you need to be reminded?" Mr. S. moved toward his desk and his grade book. "I can read off your names—"

Before he could say another word, everyone in our group scrambled out of their seats. Even though the rest of the class would know who was going as soon as we stood up—and most of them knew already—having him read our names aloud would be the ultimate humiliation. I dragged my-self out of the room, not looking at anyone, and waited for the others in the hall. Carter, KC, and the rest arrived a couple of seconds later. Everyone's faces were red and their eyes were on the floor—well, everyone except KC.

"Here we go," he proclaimed, leading the pack down the hall. "It's like a fairy tale: The Adventures of Miss Ham-Prince and the Seven Lame-Os in Tutor-land." He winked at me when he said it.

I was torn between wanting to jab him with my pencil or laugh. Although stabbing him probably would have been more satisfying, I did neither.

"Watch it, KC," Carter mumbled. I guess he didn't count himself as a lame-o. And in this fairy tale, I was going to the wrong castle. I hung at the rear of the group, trying to come up with a way to avoid TLC. Could I make myself fall down the stairs and break a leg? Slam my finger in a locker? Unfortunately, there was no way to make either option look like an accident.

KC moved to walk beside me. "Why so slow, Your Highness?"

"Knock it off, KC."

"But I only exist to serve you," he said with a bow. Ever the court jester. I cocked an eyebrow at him.

A kind of choke-cough came from behind me. I spun around to see Ty, carrying Mr. Symphony's attendance sheet, cheeks pink and eyes narrowed.

"Hey," I said to him, an uncomfortable sensation traveling through my body. Ooooh, awkward! He didn't even say anything, just gave KC a stiff nod and stalked off in the direction of the office. Dezzie would *definitely* classify that as a "display."

I wanted to run after him. But if I did that, I'd be forced to talk about "us," and I just wasn't ready for that. Torn in two, I reluctantly let him go and turned my attention back to KC, who had bounced up to the front of the group.

We made it down the stairs with everyone in one piece, and found ourselves standing outside the TLC door. Even KC quieted down. The door was decorated with large construction paper leaves, and a cheery sign proclaimed: "Need a little extra TLC in your classes? Get help here!"

We just stood there, hoping that someone else in the bunch would grab the handle first. No one had to, because it popped open from the inside.

"Hello everyone! You must be from Mr. Symphony's math class." A perky blond woman wearing a plaid skirt held the door open and waved us in. "I'm Mrs. Arbuckle, one of the parent volunteers. We're so glad to see you!"

I hadn't been in TLC since I was a sixth grader and needed to make up a test. The room hadn't changed much. Long tables ran down the center in a row, and shelves lined with books came halfway up the walls. Those encouraging posters—you know, the ones with big pictures of eagles or mountains on them, labeled with words such as "believe" and "dream"—filled every available wall. I guess it was supposed to be a positive atmosphere, but seeing those posters basically made me feel like "failure" and "disgrace."

We pulled chairs out and sat at one of the tables. Mrs. Arbuckle stood at the end.

"Since there are nine of you, you'll be split into groups of three and be assigned a TLC tutor, whom you'll work with every day for the next four weeks. We'll go over the class lectures and homework assignments. We'll even give you some solid study strategies to get you in fighting shape for that upcoming exam!" She ended with a shining smile and a boxing-style swing.

I felt kind of bad for her. No one wanted to be here, and she was trying to be as enthusiastic as possible.

"Here are your tutors," she said, gesturing. Another parent came out of the office, wearing a concerned expression and wringing her hands. I was close to wringing mine too. I hadn't seen Dezzie yet, and was afraid that she'd pop up from under a table with an "I'm the smart sister" sign around her neck.

"Excuse me, Laura?" she hissed. Mrs. Arbuckle excused herself and the two had a whispered conversation in the corner. Mrs. Arbuckle came back.

"It seems that Mr. Hsu, our other parent volunteer, has taken ill," she said. "We'll just have to put you in larger groups for today. Ms. Grafton will be working with Hamlet Kennedy, KC Rails, Julie Kennelly, and Davy Williams. I'll take the rest of you."

Wrong castle, and my prince was in another group. Just me and the fool again. The groups shuffled off to their respective tables. Still no sign of Dezzie. Maybe she'd picked up on my telepathy and disappeared.

The next second, I almost believed she *was* telepathic— and not in a good way. The door opened and Dezzie came in carrying a stack of library books. In her blue tunic and leggings, with her hair pulled back into a low ponytail, she looked like your typical seventeenth-century second grader. And until that moment, I hadn't noticed that we'd worn our hair the same way that morning. In a flash, I undid mine, trying to put some distance between us.

It didn't matter. Everyone was staring at her, including me. It was like a neon arrow that glowed "freak family" over my sister's head.

Dezzie didn't smile, wave, or acknowledge us. She just plunked her books down at the far table and sat with her back to the rest of the room. My stomach twisted as tight as a piece of licorice.

Ms. Grafton led our group to a table at the opposite corner from Dezzie, and told us to spread out. I opened my notebook and tried to concentrate as Ms. Grafton started explaining variables, but it was like Dezzie was a magnet that pulled my eyes in her direction. I wanted to know if other people were looking at her, what she was doing, if she was watching us, and, most of all, if my chances of ever blending in again were gone for good.

Ms. Grafton was also having a tough time.

"KC, I won't ask you again. Keep all four feet of your chair on the ground, please." She frowned, and that "please" wasn't said in a nice, polite way—it was clipped and short. KC's chair clicked back to the floor, then I saw him push it up again. I hid a smile behind my hand, grateful that his antics pulled me away from my Dezzie worries.

She started talking about x and y again, but my eyes—and brain—wandered. I could hear Mrs. Arbuckle's group at the next table. Someone asked a question about the value of x that I didn't understand. Evidently, Mrs. Arbuckle didn't either. She stammered a little, then leaned over and spoke to Ms. Grafton.

"Marion? Can you explain to my group how the value of x changes when . . ." And I didn't pay attention to the rest.

Either Ms. Grafton also didn't, or the question was more than she bargained for in her parent tutor duties. Her face went blank under her thick black bangs.

"We'll have to look that one up," she said, and began flipping through our textbook. Mrs. Arbuckle leaned over her shoulder.

I felt her coming up from behind me.

"The value changes because the integers . . ." Dezzie started. The two parents turned to her, as did the rest of us.

She launched into the explanation, tugging on the hem of her shirt the whole time. When she was finished, she turned and walked back to her seat without waiting for anyone's response. No one said anything for a minute.

"Oh," said Carter, finally. I guess he was the one who'd asked the question in the first place. "I get it now."

Mrs. Arbuckle and Ms. Grafton nodded.

"Um, yes. Well." It was like Mrs. Arbuckle didn't know what to do next. I mean, it *is* strange to have a small child come up to you and know the answer to the problem you're trying to solve, but you'd think adults would recover better. Dezzie clearly had thrown them for a loop. For once, I was too proud of her to be embarrassed.

"Perhaps Desdemona would be willing to help us out?" Ms. Grafton suggested to Mrs. Arbuckle as though there was no one in the room. "Just until Jim Hsu comes back."

And just like that, the humiliation returned.

Mrs. Arbuckle turned in Dezzie's direction, her lips in a funny twist.

"That's a great idea," she answered. *No it's not!* I wanted to yell. Instead, I watched helplessly as she crossed the space and sat down next to Dezzie. They spoke in low tones. The whole time, I watched Dezzie's ponytail bobbing. It moved in time to my queasy stomach.

"Didn't know they let people under four feet tall become tutors," KC whispered in my ear. "Isn't it illegal for someone that age to be working?"

I clenched my fists at my sides and tried to ignore him, but my eyes kept drifting back to his grin. It may have been responsible for the odd tingly, prickling feeling at the back of my neck. For a second—no, a *millisecond*—I wondered if he was the origami artist. Then I remembered what Dezzie said, that origami takes patience and precision. Uh-uh. No way. *Not* KC.

Mrs. Arbuckle finished her conversation with my sister and stood up.

"Attention, everyone. We are going to try an experiment. I'm sure you're all familiar with Desdemona Kennedy . . ."

Too familiar, thanks. And why did she have to call it "an experiment"? Mrs. Arbuckle continued, but all I could hear were my own jumbled thoughts mashed with irritation and embarrassment. Not only was my genius sister going to help kids in my class with math, but I was bombing so badly I was in one of the help groups too. Had I fallen into one of Dalí's bizarre landscapes? Next I'd see long-legged elephants come out of the girls' bathroom. It was even worse than the time my parents came to my fifth-grade concert, Mom in an Elizabethan collar, because we sang "Come Let Us All A-Maying Go."

I quit choir after that.

"Carter, Davy, and Chrissy will work with Desdemona. She will also be available for individual questions if we get stuck."

Davy's ears turned pink as he scooped up his notebook and pencils. I willed myself to disappear. Maybe you could say I was taking things a little too personally—after all, it wasn't my fault that Dezzie was a.) a genius or b.) tutoring people in my math class—but that's how it felt. Especially when Chrissy muttered "geek freak" under her breath as she passed my chair.

"Let's start again," said Ms. Grafton, once Dezzie's group was sitting at her table. "We'll start with basics of x and y." She explained why they were used and what they meant. Julie, who usually did pretty well in class, focused in on her explanation and appeared set on discovering all the secrets of pre-algebra.

I tried hard to listen, but found myself straining to get a glimpse of Dezzie. As embarrassed as I was, I was also anxious to know what they were doing and how my sister was as a group tutor. Meanwhile, KC stared over my head like

there was a TV there, tapping his pencil and doing everything but getting up from his chair. It was distracting me
from the distraction of watching my sister. I glared at him.

"Do you see?" Ms. Grafton asked. She looked at our
group. Julie nodded, a smile spreading across her face. I
tried to remember what Ms. Grafton had said, so I could
ask a question. Instead, I settled for a weak nod. KC didn't
even bother.

From behind me came the sound of laughter. I jumped,
then spun in my seat—I couldn't help it. Carter, Chrissy,
and Davy were giggling at something Dezzie had said.
She smiled and nodded at them. I swore I even saw her
bat her eyelashes at Carter. My Carter. I hadn't seen Carter
so much as smile at me in nearly three years, and my sister
got him to *giggle*? Grrrr.

"Hamlet?" Ms. Grafton said. "Are you with us?"

I turned around.

"Sorry," I muttered.

"Yeah, I don't want you to miss our discussion," KC
said, and tipped a fake hat at me. I grabbed the sides of
my chair and squeezed.

For the rest of the session, I didn't take my eyes off Ms.
Grafton. I forced myself to repeat her points in my head,
and did a couple of sample problems before the end to
be sure I could do the homework. It *was* a lot easier with
her help, but the effort it took me to concentrate was both
exhausting and nerve-wracking, especially because I could

hear Dezzie's group laughing every so often. KC did his part to keep my attention focused on him, if not on our session. He doodled illustrations of planes and monsters, plus giant, man-eating variables. Every time Mrs. Grafton glanced in his direction, he covered them with an arm.

When the bell rang, I shoved everything into my book bag and spun to check on Dezzie. Carter and Davy lingered at her table. She was pointing at something in the textbook, big gray eyes darting back and forth from the page to their faces. I could tell she was explaining something to them—she had the same patient expression on her face I'd seen so often. Torn between wanting to know what it was and not wanting to be seen with her, I hung back.

Davy and Carter picked their stuff up what seemed like hours later. I had to get my lunch from my locker, and I figured I'd walk with Dezzie. Based on Ty's reaction to seeing me with KC earlier in the period, I knew lunch was going to be uncomfortable. Why rush to get there? As soon as Davy and Carter walked away, she darted into the tutoring office with barely a wave.

"I have to meet my calculus teacher early," she called.

No time to talk. My heart sank. I'd just have to hope that she wouldn't tell Saber and Mauri—or anyone else—what she'd been up to this period. They didn't need more ammo in the Dezzie versus Hamlet war.

Then I remembered: Carter and KC had firepower too.

～Vii～

The pig count was up to seven. This one was made with aluminum foil—the shiniest of the bunch. *Was* it Ty? But I was telling the truth when I told Judith he couldn't do origami. The kid could barely fold a napkin, let alone elaborate Japanese animals.

"Well, I don't know what *I'd* do if *my* little sister was tutoring *me* in class," Mauri said loudly, interrupting my thoughts as I passed her on my way into the caf. "I guess I'd just die of embarrassment."

"I'd die of embarrassment if *I* had your *face*," I muttered in response. So much for keeping tutoring on the down low. I trudged to our table and plopped in my seat. This time, I didn't even bother taking my lunch out of the bag.

"Yikes," Ely said. "You look scary. Really scary."

I scowled at him.

"Dude, you're *not* helping," said Judith to him. She slid some vanilla sandwich cookies across the table to me. "Try these, Ham."

I picked one up and removed the top layer.

"The not-so-dynamic duo getting on your case again?" Ely asked. I nibbled and nodded, not wanting to look him in the eye. "Is it the math thing?"

"Yeah."

Ty just sat in his chair, eyes glued to his leftover pizza slices, not even glancing in my direction. It was obvious that he was ticked about the scene in the hallway with KC. Did Ty think I was flirting with KC or something? Ew!

I tried to calm the questions that whirled in my brain when I looked at Ty. Why did he have to like *me*? Did he even still want to be my friend? Or was this it—no more Ty and Ham, because he wanted to be more than friends and I didn't? Aarrggh!

"Ely told me what happened. How did they find out?" Judith asked. I took another one of her cookies.

"Dunno," I said. "Either Carter or KC told them. Or someone else, I guess." I licked the filling off the bottom layer. "This is about the worse eighth-grade year in history."

As if agreeing with me, Ty crumpled his lunch bag and pushed back from the table. With a muttered "Later," he stalked off.

"What gave him a sunburn?" Ely asked.

"Dunno," I said, lying, lying, lying. Judith scowled at me.

The school intercom crackled, cutting through the caf's

chatter and noise like a spoon through Jell-O. Mrs. Pearl's voice came through.

"Pardon the interruption. Hamlet Elizabeth Kennedy, please report to the front office immediately. Hamlet Kennedy, please report to the front office."

It was like someone had turned the spotlight of shame on me: The eyes of every eighth grader locked on to my table, and once the seventh graders figured out where they were staring, they joined in too. I'm sure the sixth graders were trying to figure out where the voice from the sky came from.

"Everything okay?" Ely asked as I pushed my chair back. A little too quickly. Without looking around.

It thumped into something solid behind me, and I heard an "oof!" and then felt something warm and lumpy dripping down my back and in my hair.

I looked up, right into the face of Carter Teegan. Who, instead of smelling like coconut shampoo, had a distinct cheesy aroma. Probably because he was wearing a plate full of mac 'n' cheese. Okay, not a whole plate.

The rest had fallen on me.

The caf erupted in noise: laughter, catcalls, cheers, whoops. My face was so hot, it could have melted like the warm, drippy cheese.

"Dude! Are you all right?" screeched Judith over the din. Ely's face danced in a million different directions. He was trying not to laugh. Jerk.

Ms. Finch-Bean, the day's lunch monitor, was by my side an instant later. "Are the two of you hurt?"

I was so busy with my own humiliation, I barely even looked at Carter. He was dabbing at the giant gooey spot on the front of his button-down shirt with a paper napkin.

"No," I said, mortified. "Carter, I'm really sorry. I didn't see you." I choked out the apology. Judith, meanwhile, mopped my head with napkins.

"Guess *not,*" he muttered. His words stung. He wasn't even trying to be nice about it.

"I-I'm sorry," I stuttered, eyes filling with tears. Ms. Finch-Bean patted my hand. The hoots and hollering were dying down, but just barely. If this is what happened when I was singled out in the caf, I couldn't imagine how bad it would be when I was onstage. The lights would probably fall and crush me.

"You were on your way to the office to begin with," she said. "So go. And you," she directed at Carter, "that'll come out with some soap and water. Give it to me—keep your T-shirt on—and I'll take it to the big sink in the art room. It'll be ready for you by the end of the day."

Ugh. So now I was responsible for making Carter Teegan take his clothes off in the middle of the caf. I was beyond mortified, and no longer cared that I'd been called to the office. If it was an emergency, it had better be a good one.

"Dude, I could escort you," Judith said, wadding up

cheese-clogged napkins. "You might need help after this trauma."

I shook my head. A piece of macaroni fell out of my hair and splatted onto the floor. "No thanks."

I kept my gaze on the ground, about four feet in front of where I was walking, so I wouldn't have to see everyone else staring. It didn't do anything to block out the giggles and laughter, though. Slowly, as I made my way across the room, the conversations resumed. My face was so bright, it could have lit a path in the dark.

Once out of the caf, I took a deep breath and brushed the remaining mac and cheese from my hair. It was leaving a trail down the hall. I willed myself not to cry.

Why was I being called to the office? I ran through everything I had done that morning. There was no rule I'd broken, no one I'd been in trouble with. I had nearly been late to two of my classes, and barely had time to speak with anyone in between. But now that I was covered in a dairy disaster, I was about to find out.

When I arrived at the office, things became a little clearer. Dezzie was sitting in one of the chairs next to Mrs. Pearl's desk.

"Thank you for coming so quickly, dear," Mrs. Pearl said. It was like she didn't even notice my faux-cheddar-covered head.

"Is everything okay?" I glanced at Dezzie, and her eyes grew round.

"What happened to you?" she asked.

I ignored the question. "Where's Mom?"

"She just called. Seems that she is held up at a meeting, and your sister needs to get home in time for her afternoon lessons. She excused you to walk her home," Mrs. Pearl finished. I fished a piece of pasta from the front pocket of my shirt. "Assuming, of course, that you come back when her tutor arrives at your house."

I had been called to the front office, then knocked mac and cheese all over myself and Carter Teegan in front of the whole school, because I had to walk my sister home? Did my parents have any *clue* about reality? Did my life matter at all to them? I fought the urge to scream.

Deep breath.

"Sure."

At least I could shower and change.

"I'll have someone pick up your assignments from your next class," Mrs. Pearl said as the end of lunch bell rang.

Thankfully, it wasn't math.

"Do you have your stuff?" I directed at Dezzie. She nodded, solemn.

We left the office and headed to the front of the building.

"I am sorry, Hamlet," she said when we reached the sidewalk. "I know you don't want to do this. And you're not having a very good day today."

Dezzie, Queen of the Understatement.

"No, Dezzie, I'm not." Then I shook my head, getting a whiff of orange cheddar. "It's fine. You can't stay at HoHo all day." Inside, I was screaming, "I'm covered in mac and cheese! *Mac and cheese!* And I have to walk you home?!!!"

This wasn't really about Dezzie. It was about Mom and Dad. It was about how unfair this whole situation was—Dezzie had to get what she needed, so she had to go to *my* school. *My* life was turned around too. I had to leave *my* classes to walk her home (okay, and to shower out the cheese on my head, but that wouldn't have happened if she hadn't been at HoHo). And they were so wrapped up in their Elizabethan breeches that they had no clue.

We went the rest of the way in silence, our footsteps crunching in the dry fall leaves. I didn't want to think about the caf, or pigs, or Carter, or Ty, or the coagulating goo on my neck. I just wanted this day to be over.

When we reached the house, I unlocked the door and had my sister leave a message with Mom's department secretary that we'd arrived safely. There would be no need for *me* to leave a message that I'd made it back to school, I thought with a bitter twinge. I went upstairs to get cleaned up.

After a quick shower and a change of clothes, I felt a little better—and smelled *much* better. Dezzie sat at the kitchen table, still waiting for her tutor. I poured myself a glass of milk.

"Who's coming today?" I asked.

"Professor Bigsby. Math," she said when she caught my puzzled expression. She went upstairs to get her books. I finished my drink and put my glass in the sink. Through the front window, I saw a small blue car pull up. A man with curly hair and thick glasses got out, carrying a sheaf of papers and books. I opened the door for him.

"You must be Hamlet," he said. "I'd shake your hand, but . . ." He gestured at the pile of papers with his chin.

"My sister's upstairs," I said. She came down with her books and they settled at the dining room table. I told Dezzie I'd be straight home after school, but I doubt the two of them heard me. They were already deep into math with way more letters than numbers.

And I felt like a remainder.

Two hours later, when I was going home from school for the second time that day, this time cheese-free, I heard the slap-slap-slap of extra feet behind me. When I turned my head, Saber and Mauri were right there.

"Aren't you going to say hi?" asked Saber, a big grin on her face and her ponytail bouncing.

"Are you lost?" They drew up next to me. Mauri laughed.

"That's too funny!" she cried. They matched their steps with mine.

"Is it me, or does something smell like cheddar?" Mauri said. Her nails were painted bright blue.

174

"Hmmm. Must be your breath," I replied.

"Nice job, knocking into Carter," said Saber. "Do you have a *crash* on him?"

"Get lost," I snapped, and picked up my pace. I had no more desire to play nice.

"We're visiting someone," Saber said, ignoring my direction and speeding up to stay with me.

"In your neighborhood," Mauri added. I could guess who.

"Why?" They looked at me like I'd sprouted nine heads.

"Because she's our *friend*," Saber said. She rolled her eyes. "And she said we could come over."

"She did?" I stopped in my tracks. Dezzie hadn't mentioned anything to me about inviting them to our house. They nodded. "Well, my parents are at a meeting," I said, thinking fast. The last people I wanted to hang out with at home after a day like today was *them*. "My mom doesn't like it when we have people over when they're not there." It was a lie—they didn't mind if Ty, Judith, or Ely came by when they were at work. But Dezzie'd never had anyone but tutors to the house.

Mauri and Saber glanced at each other.

"My mom is going to pick us up at your house," Saber said. "She's coming at four. Can't we just hang out until we get there?"

We were at the corner of our street. Mauri and Saber

had expectant looks on their faces. I remembered Dezzie saying how she never had school friends before.

"I guess so." May as well put a fork in this whole day—it was done. I turned down the street without waiting for their response. Having Saber Greene and Mauri Lee in my house was like inviting a wolf in for a steak dinner.

I opened the front door and called out to Dezzie. When she appeared around the corner, her eyes widened. Iago was right behind her, all wagging tail and licking kisses. Traitor.

"Hi," she said, sounding shy.

Saber and Mauri pushed past me. They squealed over how "cute" our house was and how "adorable" Iago was and asked Dezzie for a "tour." I trailed behind as Dezzie showed them around, trying not to retch.

"Oh look at these! Are they your relatives?" Mauri asked. "We have pictures of my great-grandma in our house too." We were standing in the living room, in front of a display of photos of our family in costume that our parents had developed in black and white.

"No," Dezzie said. "They were taken at King George's Faire. We do a family portrait there every summer." Saber and Mauri leaned closer. Iago sat on his velvet pillow and began licking his paws.

"I bet we'll learn a lot about your parents when they come to class," Mauri said. "I mean, *from* your parents." Saber nudged her.

"Oh, that *is* you," Saber said, picking up one of the frames. "You look so cute wearing that dress. What's that your dad's holding?"

"A mead flagon," Dezzie replied, as though it was the most natural thing in the world.

"Did Shakespeare use mead flagons?" Mauri must have seen my skeptical expression, because she followed up her question with a snide, "What? We're doing research on his life for English class." Um, yeah.

"Yes," Dezzie answered, ignoring my scowl.

Their little "tour" was excruciating. It was like Saber and Mauri had radar for anything Shakespearean or strange, and that's what they would ask questions about, all "for the sake of research." And no matter how many times I tried to catch Dezzie's eye for an "I told you so" glare, she just ignored me.

From the photos, to the heavy goblets Mom kept in the china cabinet, to the two antique candleholders on the mantel, they pointed all of them out. Even things that I'd never considered odd—like our boot scraper or the piles of books everywhere—they honed in on. More than anything, I wished for an average home with an average family—one where there was a microwave, or where the TV set wasn't on wheels and turned to face the wall most of the time. One where the parents didn't debate the origins of the word "wench" at the dinner table. One where you didn't get covered in mac and cheese because your sister needed an escort home. One where someone like me could fit in and matter.

We'd traipsed upstairs.

"Do you want to see the replica Red Chinese Army costume I made last year?" Dezzie asked the girls. Saber and Mauri shot an amused look over Dezzie's head. I'd had enough. I ducked into my own room without waiting for their response.

A short time later, I heard them clomp down to the basement. I imagined them gawking at Mom's Shakespeare collection, or asking Dezzie what "Fair is foul, and foul is fair" and "There's small choice in rotten apples" meant when they saw the quotes stitched on our throw pillows. I wanted to both hide under my bed and yell at them for coming here and making fun of my family. Instead, I spread my homework across my comforter and paged through the assignments I had to finish, hoping for distraction.

I had to write my essay—work on math, read for science, answer history questions on Elizabethan England, and finish making the players Ty and I would use to stage the scene in our Globe. But all that came to mind were the cheese in my hair and the look on Ty's face when he split at lunch earlier. He hadn't waited for me at the quad after school either. I'm sure he'd heard about what happened in the caf. Did he not care? Was he that mad about what KC had said? *Was* he my locker stalker? He could have learned origami through some online tutorial thing. Even though I didn't want to believe it was him, it *was* possible. Obviously, this whole situation with his feelings—and my lack of feelings for him—was a bigger problem than I wanted to admit. I needed to talk to him, but the thought made me ill. He was like my brother, and with my sister hanging out with the Gruesome Twosome, there was no one left for me.

The house had grown quiet. Then the doorbell clanged. On autopilot, I left my bedroom and went downstairs.

Dezzie, Saber, and Mauri appeared in the front hall at the same time as me. The bell rang again. I stopped where I was, allowing Dezzie to answer, but didn't leave.

"I've got it, Hamlet," she said, glaring at me. The intensity of her stare made me step back. Saber and Mauri were huddled behind her, whispering.

"Fine," I muttered, clearly seeing that I wasn't wanted. I took my time making my way up the steps. Dezzie opened the door.

"Oh hello." Mrs. Greene's voice floated up to the second-floor landing, where I was listening. "Is Desdemona home? Or maybe your mom or dad?"

To stop myself from laughing out loud, I bit the heel of my left hand. I could only imagine how red Dezzie's face was, standing in front of this grown-up she could think hexagons around.

Dezzie's reply was too soft for me to hear everything,

but I caught a few very firm words. Next, Mauri's and Saber's voices found their way to my perch. But again, I couldn't tell what they were saying.

What I *did* hear, though, were feet pounding back down to the basement. Saber's and Mauri's feet, I realized—I could hear Dezzie chatting with Mrs. Greene. Maybe one of the girls had left her personality behind? The thought nearly started me laughing again, so I chomped on my hand for a second time.

After a minute or two, they came back to the first floor, slower than when they'd went down. Murmured good-byes, then the front door clicked closed. As quietly as I could, I scooted back to my bedroom. I heard Dezzie go back into the basement.

"How'd it go?" I asked a little while later, on my way to the kitchen for a drink. Iago was stretched out on the rug, snoozing. I stepped over him. Dezzie sat in the den, the History Channel on, a book open in her lap and two more on the coffee table. Staring off into space, she wasn't paying attention to any of it. She shrugged.

"Satisfactorily, I suppose. They had much interest in the Shakespeare collection," she said quickly. She drummed her fingers on the edge of the coffee table.

"Of course," I muttered, disgusted. I wanted to grab her and yell, *They're stealing off you so they don't have to do the work on their own!*

Dezzie picked at a dark smudge on one of her usually spotless hands and tucked both hands underneath her when she noticed me watching.

"What?" she snapped. "They are enjoying the play very much."

Oh, yeah. Hanging out with Dezzie was making Saber and Mauri more into school than clothes. Doubtful. Very doubtful. I got my drink and went upstairs.

During dinner, Mom thanked me for walking Dezzie home.

"It was a department meeting; neither of us could get away," she explained. I nodded and said nothing, even though my anger still burned. I was sick of being pushed to the side—like my work was less important than Dezzie's, my life was less important than Dezzie's . . . my *everything* was less important than Dezzie's. As though reading my mind, Dad put down the papers he was grading and spoke up.

"This will not be a regular occurrence, Hamlet. You need to be present for your own classes, just as your sister needs to be present for her tutors. In the future, your mother and I will be more responsible about scheduling these meetings."

Although his words were what I thought I wanted to hear, they didn't help much. Usually my parents were good about keeping their promises, but when it came to Dezzie the bets were off and the macaroni flew.

"Not like it matters," I muttered under my breath.

"What was that?" my father said. I rarely sassed my parents, and surprised myself with the comment.

"Nothing," I said.

"I believe Hamlet has something to say," my mother remarked in her annoying professor tone. She put her fork down. "Speak now, as you have our full attention."

Across from me, Dezzie's eyes bounced back and forth between my parents like someone playing a video game. Not that she'd ever *seen* one, let alone played one.

"Dezzie's being used!" I blurted, the sentence releasing pressure that I'd been carrying around for weeks. Where had *that* come from? Instead of shouting about the unfairness of my life, I was trying to protect my sister.

Mom frowned at my use of Dezzie's nickname.

"By whom?" Dad asked. He ate another forkful of pickled-whatever-Mom-made.

"These two girls at school," I said, relief sweeping through me.

"Is this true, Desdemona?" Mom's asked, face poised in concern.

Dezzie shook her head. "Two of my peers are very invested in their education," she said. "I believe that their questions show a marked interest in the Bard and they are not acting in a superficial manner due to my intellect."

Mom and Dad nodded, taking Dezzie's word over mine.

"Well, be sure that you encourage them to do their

own work and synthesize their own ideas of the text," Dad responded. Dezzie gave them a wide grin.

"And *you*"—my mother turned to me—"be sure of what you speak."

How was this happening? I figured they'd go through the roof when they heard what was happening to their genius-baby, but it was like I was the one who was doing something wrong. They hadn't heard me at all.

"And he goes through life, his mouth open, and his mind closed," I said, using one of Dad's favorite Shakespeare quotes.

"And doing all of the dishes this evening," my mother retorted. "That is enough impudence from you, young lady."

With a scowl, I pushed back from the table and went into the kitchen. But I kept my mouth firmly closed. Talking to them would *never* do any good. They'd forever keep Dezzie front and center, while I was relegated to the wings. Or, I thought, with a twinge of irony, to stagehand.

∽Viii∽

few days later, it was time for me to read again in English. I intended to do the same halting, word-by-word rendition I'd done the last time, hoping against all hope that Mrs. Wimple would change her mind and force Puck on some other unfortunate soul.

This period, I was reading the part of Titania, queen of the fairies. Puck had given her a love potion and she'd fallen for Bottom, whose head had been turned into a donkey's. Even though he looked—and acted—completely ridiculous, Titania didn't see it. She couldn't.

If only real life were as simple as Shakespeare life: potions and fairies instead of messy feelings and friendships. But it was a cool plot line, and I kind of got caught up in the story. So caught up, I forgot to stumble through my part.

"Be kind and courteous to this gentleman;/Hop in his walks and gambol in his eyes;/Feed him with apricocks and dewberries,/With purple grapes, green figs, and mulberries;/The honey-bags steal from the humble-bees,/

And for night-tapers crop their waxen thighs . . ." The words rolled off my tongue so easily, I was barely aware that I was reading them. I kind of saw the story playing out in my head, absorbing the meaning of the words as I went along. Titania wanted the fairies to take perfect care of Bottom, treating him like a king. I finished the line and waited for Julie Kennelly, playing Peaseblossom, to come in. She didn't.

I glanced up. The whole class was staring at me.

"Ms. Kennedy," Mrs. Wimple said, her words as crisp as burnt toast, "I applaud your mature decision to embrace your talent."

I opened my mouth to tell her that I hadn't decided on any part of this, but realized I'd be better off not saying anything. I closed it again. Mrs. Wimple glanced at the clock.

"A word before you leave," she said. "Next week, we have some special guests coming in to help us develop a better understanding of Shakespeare's language. The doctors Kennedy—Hamlet's parents—will be paying us a visit. I expect you'll all be on your best behavior."

My body instantly flashed hot, then icy cold. I broke out in a sweat. My parents. Were. Coming. To. School. It was bound to happen eventually, but I hoped that it wouldn't. Or that a volcano would erupt in Boston, smothering school, Shakespeare, and everything that went with them in black ash.

It was real. Ty raised an eyebrow at me. My belly cork-screwed like the binding of a spiral notebook.

The bell rang, and everyone scooped up their books.

"Ms. Kennedy," Mrs. Wimple said. Her after-class summonses were getting old.

The classroom emptied, and I took my time gathering my things and crossing the space to her desk. I tried to act calm, but my thoughts jumped and danced faster than any Shakespeare fairy ever could. Why-why-*why* did they have to come in? Was there any way I could play sick?

I was so tied up in my own agony that I never considered Mrs. Wimple's mood.

"*That* last stanza was quite different from how you read prior to today," she said, staring straight at me. Future parental humiliation forgotten, I dropped my eyes to the floor.

"Uh," I mumbled, hoping that she'd accept that the last bit had been an accident or something. She put on her patented brain X-ray stare.

"I kind of got into it, I guess," I admitted, sick of lying and suddenly more worried about my parents than my reading. *And remember how it feels when you practice?* a little voice in my head chirped. I liked how easily the words came to me . . .

"It's about time," Mrs. Wimple said.

The late bell buzzed.

She scribbled a note on the pass and slid it across the

top of her desk, then turned away from me as I picked it up and bolted.

By the time I made it to pre-al, I was ten minutes late. I crept into the class, hoping to slip into my seat, but the desks were in a circle and Mr. Symphony was bent over, talking quietly to someone on the far side. There was nowhere for me to go.

"Miss Kennedy," he said, straightening, "shouldn't you be somewhere else?""

For a second, I thought he was sending me to the principal's office or back to James, the counselor. I couldn't breathe and was frozen to the spot.

"TLC, Miss Kennedy?" he said, when I didn't respond.

Relief swept through me.

"Sorry," I muttered, and fled the room.

I didn't have time to lean against any walls or hide out in the girls' bathroom. By the time I reached TLC, I'd gotten myself together and my breathing was more regular. I pushed the door open and slipped in. My hand still clutched the late pass.

The three tutors were seated at different tables. Mrs. Arbuckle's was closest to the door. She was pointing at something in the textbook. Her group was in the varying positions of bored—staring at the ceiling, tapping pencils, yawning.

Ms. Grafton sat between KC and Julie. By the way her mouth was pulled into a tight line, it was clear that she was having a hard time with one of them. Guess who?

Dezzie was on the far side of the room. Carter, Chrissy, and Davy were staring at her with these amazed expressions on their faces, like she was the most interesting person they'd ever met. Dezzie's hands were flitting in front of her face, butterfly-like, and she'd stop and point back to the book every so often.

I stood in the doorway and watched for a minute or two. Carter smiled and nodded, then smacked his forehead with the palm of his hand in an "I can't believe I didn't realize that" gesture. His brilliant grin made my heart pound harder. Dezzie laughed. It was obvious that they were learning stuff from her, but it also seemed like they were having fun.

How had my sister, who hadn't followed any of my crucial-to-middle-school rules, become *popular*? Because this attention wasn't the sneaky Saber/Mauri interest, this was genuine. These kids *liked* her. *Carter* liked her.

"Hamlet?" Ms. Grafton's voice cut into my thoughts. I snapped my head in her direction. Everyone else in the room snapped their heads in mine. I swore I could feel Carter's eyes on my face like clover-colored lasers. I'm sure all he was thinking about was the mac 'n' cheese fiasco. I wanted to apologize again, but I felt about as capable of doing that as I did juggling knives—but considering my recent track record with odd talents, who knows?

"You may join us," she said. "No need to wait for an invitation."

"Yeah, Ham 'n' Cheese," KC called, "come on down!" Blushing and furious, I crossed the space and put my stuff down next to Julie, across from KC—which was as far away as I could get. Without saying anything, I slid the late pass across the table to Ms. Grafton.

There was barely enough time left in the period for me to get a fast overview of the day's assignment and do a couple of practice homework problems. Of course, the whole time Ms. Grafton was helping me, KC kicked me under the table and doodled. I tucked my legs up on the seat so they'd be out of reach, but he just switched to thumping the bottom of my chair. I didn't want to tell Ms. Grafton, so I just gritted my teeth and tried to concentrate on the math work. At least it took my mind off Dezzie's skyrocketing social status a few seats away.

When the bell buzzed, I pushed back from the table and gave KC the dirtiest look I could. He smiled like a freckle-covered angel, and I felt my death stare soften a little. Ugh! *Why?!*

Ms. Grafton tousled his hair.

"You made me earn my keep today," she said, smiling back at him. Moment of softness over, I wanted to throw up in the potted plant in the corner. However, seeing if Dezzie's mysterious ability held up through the whole class period was more important. She'd totally blown off my rules, but, in spite of it, was she actually blending in?

KC bumped against me as he was leaving and slipped something into my hand. When I opened my palm, there was a scrap of paper bearing a teeny drawing of a top-hat-wearing, dancing ham (the actual meat, not me). Against my better judgment, I grinned.

From behind me, I heard Dezzie saying good-bye. I stashed the picture in my backpack, and when I turned around, Carter was lingering at her table. I shifted from foot to foot, not wanting to embarrass myself even more by breaking into their conversation. They finished, Carter slung his backpack over one shoulder, and headed for the door. He passed so close to me I could smell coconuts.

I wanted to bury my head in the sand. "About the other day . . ."

"Oh. Yeah. Whatever. She's amazing," he said, giving his head a shake. I finally got up the nerve to say *something* to Carter Teegan, even though it was another apology—and right away he has to mention my *sister*. I tried not to be annoyed, focusing instead on his overall cuteness. "I get this stuff now," he sighed as happily as my mother after a Maypole dance.

I nodded and made an "uh-huh" noise, breathing in his tropical smell—a big improvement over the cafeteria cheddar.

Dezzie was packing up her books, sliding them into her bag, when I reached her.

"Hey," she said, glancing at me.

"Hey." Now that I had her attention, I didn't know how to approach her. It was hard to come out and say "Now do you see the difference between this group and the Mooch Twins?" Her books stowed away, she hitched her bag on her shoulder, staring at me all the while.

"Did you want to ask me something?" she wondered.

"Uh, not really," I said, chickening out. I searched for something else to say. "How's tutoring going?" We were walking in step from the classroom.

"Satisfactorily. Carter and Davy are picking things up very quickly. Chrissy is too. I am using your instructions on how to fit in socially."

"That's good," I responded, pleased in spite of myself that Dezzie might be employing some of my advice after all. I fiddled with the strap on my book bag.

"Why were you late?" she asked.

Everything that happened in English flashed through my mind: the forced reading, the moment when I found myself enjoying the play, Mrs. Wimple's comments, the fact that Mom and Dad would be coming to school . . . a wave of overwhelming stress crashed over me. Would she even get it? Definitely not the part about Mom and Dad. But I could ask her what she thought of being different . . . if it was hard for her to be so smart around people that were her own age—or, in her case—older? If standing out from the crowd was something she liked, or had just gotten used to?

The questions simmered on the surface of my brain like bubbling spaghetti sauce, but there was no way I was going to ask them out loud. Doing that meant that I believed that I had a Shakespeare-spouting gift, and a.) I still didn't want to believe it, and b.) even if I did believe it, I didn't want to admit it. Not even to Dezzie.

↻ iX ↺

That Friday night, my mom cornered me after dinner.

"Hamlet, what are your plans for the weekend?" She picked some lint off her giant fuzzy sweater.

I needed to work on my English and history, plus study pre-al and answer some science questions—nothing that I wanted to do. But there was a fine line: Admit to a lot of homework and be stuck in my room all weekend, or say that I didn't have much going on and open myself up to the horrors that lurked as "family time" with my parents. And I'd be getting enough of that next week. In class.

"I have *some* homework," I answered, hoping that a middle-of-the-road response would get me out of whatever she had planned.

"I see. Well, your sister would like to go to the mall this weekend, and I was hoping you could go with her."

"Desdemona wants to go to the mall?"

It seemed that Saber and Mauri had invited Dezzie after all. I wondered if they'd be in for another classic Kennedy mall moment?

Dezzie hadn't set foot in any shopping center since the Christmas she was three, when we went as a family to pick out a new sewing machine for Gram. A woman dressed as an elf outside of Santa's Village bent over and asked if "the itty-bitty pwetty girl wanted to sit on Santa's lap and ask for 'pwesents.'"

"I do not sit on the laps of strangers and beg for inconsequential toys, you cretin," Dezzie had responded. She hadn't yet learned appropriate language boundaries. The memory of the expression on the elf's face at Dezzie's teensy pipsqueaky tell-off still cracked me up.

Of course, during that same trip, Dad got lost in the women's coat section of a department store and we had to have him paged.

"I don't—do not—want to bring her," I said, hoping my mother would tell Dezzie that the plan was off, still irritated that she'd ignored my warning about what Saber and Mauri were up to.

She sighed and picked at more wool. "That is unfortunate. I believe this marks an important social step for your sister, and without your involvement I shall be obliged to chaperone."

I made it nearly all the way to my room before the impact of what my mother said hit me. If I didn't go to the mall with Saber and Mauri, she would. *My mother.*

I took the stairs two at a time and raced back to Mom's study.

"I appreciate your willingness to support her in this endeavor," my mother said.

How could anyone mistake fear and resentment for willingness?

The Scene: *Shoppers Town Mall, Saturday afternoon. Saber and Mauri each have one arm linked through Dezzie's, I trail behind them.*

Saber (over Dezzie's head): I think Dez needs some sparkle, don't you?

Mauri: Absolutely.

They enter Rhinestones, the accessories store. The amount of glitter and pink glowing in the doorway is overwhelming.

Me (wanting to poke my eyes out): I think I'll wait outside.

Several minutes pass. They emerge, carrying pink bags. Dezzie wears a confused expression.

Dezzie: But why are we to wear the same nail polish on Monday? And, if we are to do so, why do we each need our own bottle? Wouldn't it be more cost effective to buy one and share it amongst ourselves?

Saber: You are too funny! This way we *all*

have it, *all* the time! *(rolls eyes over Dezzie's head at Mauri)*

Mauri: Let's go to Konnexion next. They have such cute stuff. You could get some . . . different shirts.

Dezzie tugs at her maroon tunic.

Saber: Totally. *(over shoulder to me)* Hamlet, you don't have to come *every*where with us, you know.

Me: Trust me, I'd prefer not to.

Dezzie: But our parents were insistent on the point. I think her walking behind us is a good compromise, don't you?

(Saber and Mauri laugh like this is the funniest thing they've ever heard. I fight the urge to strangle them. All of them.)

Mauri: You bet.

Me (dragging my feet the whole way): . . .

Luckily, I managed to convince Mom that I needed some social time with my friends too. Judith met me at the Chilly Spoon when we got back.

"How'd it go?" she asked. She nibbled at her black raspberry cone.

I dropped my head into my hands and groaned. "Annoying. Lame. Ridiculous. They treated her like a pet."

We dissected the whole excursion, down to the nail

polish color they picked out, and ultimately agreed that it was just one more way for Saber and Mauri to stay on Dezzie's good side until the project was done. Why couldn't she see the truth? It hurt my head.

"Speaking of projects, have you and Ely finished your Globe?"

Judith shook her head. "Dude, our second level collapsed last weekend. *Some*one didn't think we needed supports under the balcony." We munched our cones in silence for a minute.

"So . . ." Judith said. She tore the remaining wrapper off her cone and bit the bottom. I watched as she drained it of any bits of ice cream. "Not to change the subject, but . . ." She raised an eyebrow.

"No."

"No?"

"No." I squirmed in my chair. "It's just so *weird*, Judith. You don't get it. He's like my brother. I don't even know how to bring it up with him."

"Well, you'd better do it soon," she said. "He's been really upset lately."

The mango sorbet I'd eaten churned in my stomach. "Yeah. Well, I'm upset too," I snapped.

Judith shrugged. "I know. But I'm so just the messenger," she said. "I didn't *make* him like you. It's not like I have fairy dust in my pocket or anything. I'm just telling you what he said."

"What, exactly, did he say again?" We'd been through it a thousand times already, but I had to make sure I knew exactly what happened.

Judith sighed. "I told you before: We were IM'ing. He asked me if you liked anyone. I said I didn't know. He asked if I was sure. I said yes. I asked him why—did he know if someone liked you. He didn't respond. Then he said, 'Don't tell Hamlet. She'll freak out.'"

I was definitely freaking out.

"And dude, what's up with you and KC?"

"Me and KC?" I gasped, and a piece of cone shot down my throat and felt like it lodged in my lung. Judith waited through my coughing fit. "There is no 'me and KC.'"

"Um, yeah. Sure," she said, while I wiped my streaming eyes. "He is so into you."

"Whatever," I said, waving her words away and fighting a bloom of warmth at my cheeks. "Carter isn't."

"Carter Teegan is a vapid pretty boy," Judith said, voice sharp. "He's not interesting at all, just nice to look at—like . . ." She leaned way over the table toward me. "Like . . . like *meringue.*"

I burst out laughing. "Meringue. Really?"

"Really, dude. Fluffy, pretty, but no substance."

When my giggles quieted, I opened my mouth to argue, but was surprised to find I had nothing to say. He really was kind of a meringue—and I didn't even *like* meringue.

***

After the mall excursion, there was a new equation in my life: The more popular Dezzie became with Carter the Meringue, the less I was interested in him:

> **The Scene:** *In class with Carter, any day after tutoring. Teacher droning on at the board in the background.*
>
> **Carter:** Seriously, this kid *rocks*. I get pre-algebra now.
>
> **Mark Sloughman** (picking at a hangnail): Uh-huh.
>
> **Carter:** No, really. Dude. She's great.
>
> **Mark:** Yeah. Cool. You get it now.
>
> **Carter** (frustrated): You don't get it. (*turning to me*) Ham, tell him. She's awesome.
>
> **Me** (no longer fazed by the smell of coconut shampoo): . . . Uh-huh. She's great. Sure.

Saber and Mauri invited her to eat lunch with them again too. Much to my irritation, Dezzie asked Mom and accepted. On the day I knew she would be in the caf, I took my lunch to the library, claiming to Ty and the rest that I needed to work on my English assignment. Based on their expressions, nobody was fooled. Ty even tried to get me to stay by saying we had to talk about the last steps on our Globe Theatre. I told him we'd get to it later.

Still, it was easier sitting in the library, with only the librarian and a seventh grader making up a Spanish test, than suffering through a whole lunch period watching Dezzie sit at Mauri and Saber's table and wondering what they were stealing from her—or trying not to be awkward around Ty and keeping an eye out for KC's antics (*wait—could those be considered* displays*?!? Eeeek!*). Even though it seemed that Dezzie was finding her own way to fit in at HoHo, part of me wanted to protect her. The other—bigger—part was nuttier than Mom's almond ginger bread over the whole thing.

A few days after the English class incident, we were in art working on surrealist-inspired drawings. Ms. Finch-Bean had us keep a dream journal, and we were going to pick random elements from our dreams and try to connect them in a sketch.

"I had a dream about all those Shakespeare figurines at your house," Saber said to Dezzie and me. "They came to life and were chasing me through the mall."

"Eww! Total nightmare!" squealed Mauri. I glowered at them. "You can draw him and make his neck wrap all big and sticky-outy."

Dezzie put her pencil down. "It's called an Elizabethan collar."

"Whatever it's called, it's scary," Saber said. "Speaking of scary, I felt like we were being stalked at the mall last weekend. There was this lonely shadow following us around . . ." She let the last part drift off. Mauri picked up.

"So sad. So ghostly—like she has no friends." My blood boiled hotter than molten glass.

"Having no friends would be better than spending time with cheats like you," I hissed.

"My mother instructed her to accompany me," Dezzie explained, trying to defuse the discussion, but not fully comprehending what was going on. "And Hamlet, I told you, they're *not* cheating—"

"Liar!" said Mauri, a little too loud. She, Saber, and Dezzie were all staring at me angrily. Too bad. I was ticked, telling the truth, and at least two of them knew it.

Ms. Finch-Bean prevented our "conversation" from escalating. She checked our dream journals (which she wasn't reading, just making sure we wrote in them) and our image list.

"Table four, it looks to me like you've forgotten that you should be using your pencils right now, not your voices." She frowned at us. Dezzie turned pink and picked up her pencil in a hurry. She wasn't used to being scolded by anyone, let alone a teacher.

"Sorry, Ms. Finch-Bean," she mumbled, and got back to work.

"We were discussing our assignment," Saber said, "and how much we love it." Her voice was thick and sweet like honey. I wanted to swat her like a bee.

"This is not the time for discussion," Ms. Finch-Bean said. "Which I distinctly remember saying at the beginning of the period when I gave you directions. Now, work quietly or I'll split you up." She turned away from our table to continue making her rounds.

Mauri, meanwhile, seemed oblivious to Mrs. Finch-Bean's remark. Her eyebrows knitted together tighter than a sweater; the scowl on her face could have blasted the new paint off the walls.

"Jerk," Mauri spat, continuing her tirade toward me. Ms. Finch-Bean's back stiffened. She had bent over to tie her shoe just a few feet away.

"Stop! We'll get in trouble," whispered Saber, one eye on the teacher . . . who spun toward us.

"Who said that?" she snapped, green eyes darkening like a stormy sea. She scanned each of our faces. She was so angry, I could *feel* her eyes crawling over me. "That language is unacceptable in the classroom, and particularly unacceptable in reference to a teacher!"

Everyone else in the class froze, forgotten pencils or notebooks clutched in their hands. No one bothered to hide the fact that they were staring at us.

My shoulders knotted and crept up somewhere around my ears. Ms. Finch-Bean thought Mauri called *her* a jerk! I waited for Mauri to say something, to apologize and explain, but all she was doing was giving Ms. Finch-Bean this tight little smile.

"Well?" Ms. Finch-Bean said again. "I'm waiting for an answer." She crossed her arms and glared at us. Dezzie shifted on her stool.

I wasn't going to be the one to tell her who said it, although nothing would have made me happier than to see Mauri get in trouble.

The bell buzzed. Behind us, the other kids in class shot uneasy glances at one another.

"You may pack up your journals and leave," Ms. Finch-Bean said without turning around. Without talking, they stuffed their backpacks and put their materials away. At our table, Saber reached down to grab her bag.

"Not you," said Ms. Finch-Bean. "You four aren't going anywhere until I get an answer." Saber's bag thunked to the ground.

I'd be missing the beginning of English. As the tension around our table increased, though, those awful readings of *A Midsummer Night's Dream* seemed as desirable as a Chilly Spoon Strawberry Shortcake Supreme Sundae. I'd read beautifully for a thousand years to avoid this situation.

Mauri studied her nail polish. Of the four of us, she was the only one who appeared unconcerned by the whole situation. Anger swept through me again.

"This type of rudeness is against school policy," Ms. Finch-Bean said. "And it will be dealt with as such. Now, which of you said it, or do I have to bring *all* of you to see Principal Obin?"

At the mention of the principal, Dezzie stiffened in her seat. For the first time, I noticed her hands, gripping the edge of the table. Her knuckles were white.

"Ms. Finch-Bean . . ." she started. Her voice was small and barely audible. Mauri turned toward her like a shark going after a seal. Dezzie pretended not to notice. She cleared her throat. "It was—" Next to me, Saber flinched. Mauri must have kicked her. Other kids arrived at the room. By their size and the way they hung at the edge of the doorway, I guessed they were sixth graders.

"Don't try to cover for her," Saber said, patting Dezzie's hand and avoiding my eyes.

"Cover for whom?" Ms. Finch-Bean stepped closer to our table. "Tell me, Miss Greene."

The late bell buzzed. Ms. Finch-Bean glanced around her next class as though she'd forgotten they were coming.

"We'll take this into the hall, then. Go out there and wait for me—all four of you." We snagged our bags and trudged to the hall. The tension in my shoulders and neck built to a piercing headache. This was like the anti–Chilly Spoon treat: The Sundae of Stress. It contained scoops of my parents' impending visit and imminent discovery of my reading ability, the Ty situation, and Dezzie getting played by these homework mooches—and now the trip to the principal's office served as the cherry on top. I tried to scoot between Saber and Mauri to tell Dezzie to leave things alone, but they jammed close to her sides and blocked me.

"Guys," I whispered, my voice sounding like a dry croak. Maybe we could agree on a way to present the situation to Ms. Finch-Bean that wouldn't get us in any more trouble than we already were. Saber and Mauri ignored me. The two of them were using a mixture of silent eye communication, gestures, and what was probably telepathy to figure out what to do next. And I was left out of the loop.

Why wouldn't Mauri just confess to the mistake? If she and Saber hadn't started the whole stupid argument by making fun of me in the first place, this wouldn't have happened. I was more than angry—I was furious as a fairy queen who finds out she's in love with a jackass.

Dezzie leaned one side against the wall, back to us all, head tilted to the ceiling. I was pretty sure she was trying not to cry. But her obliviousness was giving Saber and Mauri time to concoct a two-person plan of attack. My stomach sank. I tried to grab Dezzie's arm, to spin her around to face me, but Saber slid between us.

"Leave her alone," she said through gritted teeth, eyes out for Ms. Finch-Bean. "Can't you see she's *upset*?"

"Who isn't?" I shot back.

Beyond Saber, I could see Mauri whispering in Dezzie's ear. The door squeaked and Ms. Finch-Bean came into the hall like she'd been a drill sergeant in another life—back straight, face grim, no smile whatsoever in her eyes.

"With me." We obeyed, falling into line behind her. I'd never seen a teacher so angry—not even Mrs. Pyll in fourth grade after Mark Sloughman glued her desk drawers shut and she couldn't get her car keys.

I caught Mauri whispering "Major mad-itude," to Saber, and although I didn't find the joke funny, the description was accurate. There was some mega mad-itude coming off Ms. Finch-Bean, for sure.

"No talking!" Ms. Finch-Bean barked. Even Mauri kept quiet after that. We walked the rest of the way in silence.

What seemed like a second later, we were sitting in the row of chairs next to Mrs. Pearl's desk. I couldn't help but think that each time I'd been in the front office this term—and it was only eight weeks old!—I'd been there with my sister: her schedule, walking her home, and now this. They say the third time for anything is a charm, but this was more like a curse. Until this year, I'd only been to the office if I was sick (once), or dropping something off for a teacher (rarely).

Ms. Finch-Bean disappeared behind the principal's door. Again, Saber and Mauri had worked it so that Dezzie sat between them. If I wanted to talk to her, I had to lean across Saber to do it . . . and as soon as I started to shift forward, Saber suddenly had something important to say to Mauri. Or Dezzie. And her voice was too low for me to hear.

The office door opened, springing Ms. Finch-Bean. She didn't even give us a glance as she blew by, walking with long strides to get back to her waiting class.

"Mauri Lee," Principal Obin's voice boomed from the open door, "I'd like to see you now."

Mauri and Saber exchanged knowing glances and she went into the room and closed the door. My stomach spun and I fought the urge to grab Dezzie and bolt. Without Mauri, Saber didn't seem nearly as cool or comfortable— she picked at her sparkly sheer nail polish and kept sending nervous glances to the door. And with an open seat next to my sister, I took my chance.

I thumped into the chair harder than I'd wanted, making it clack against the wall. Dezzie didn't seem to notice. Saber leaned across her to show me her scowl. Mrs. Pearl, on the phone with a talker who, based on the reassuring noises Mrs. Pearl was making, was clearly an unhappy parent, left us alone.

"What're you going to tell him?" I whispered in Dezzie's ear.

"The truth." She didn't meet my eyes.

Principal Obin's door opened again, and Mauri stepped out. Her face was paler than when she went in, and although I studied her face for any giveaways that there'd been tears, I didn't see any. She noticed me watching and sneered.

"Desdemona Kennedy," the voice boomed. Beside me,

Dezzie cringed. She grabbed her book bag and moved past Mauri to go in. She never took her eyes off the floor.

With Dezzie gone, I was left alone with Saber and Mauri, who had to wait for Mrs. Pearl to hang up and write out her late pass.

"What happened? Is he going to call our parents?" Saber's voice quaked with what sounded like barely controlled fear. As much as I didn't want to admit it, I sympathized. Besides, now I had a whole new worry—that the school would call Mom and Dad. How would *they* react?

"Why didn't you tell Ms. Finch-Bean the truth?" I snapped at Mauri. "This is *your* fault."

"Leave it alone, cheesehead," Mauri hissed. "No one is saying *any*thing."

"But we didn't *do* anything," I said. "You're being ridiculous."

"Prove it," she said. I faltered—how could I prove it? She must have read the indecision on my face. "See. You can't. So just keep quiet or Prinicpal Obin will think you or your brainiac sister lost control of her mouth."

"Is that a threat?" I said, anger rising through my anxiety.

Instead of answering, Mauri tossed her head toward the far side of the room, near the teachers' mailboxes. Saber scooted off her seat to follow her. The two of them huddled and had a quick whispered conversation. Every once in a while, their eyes would float in my direction. I was betting that they were making sure that Saber told the same story to Principal Obin, and with me and Dezzie it would be a we said/they said situation. Who would he believe? The oddly named sisters, one of whom is a genius and the other who can't pass math, or the two cute, normal girls? What would happen to us if he didn't believe the truth?

Mrs. Pearl brought her conversation to an end, and before she hung up, Saber was back in her chair. Mauri politely asked for a late pass.

The door opened again. Dezzie emerged, smiling, relief plastered across her face like a billboard.

"Saber Greene."

Her face *was* green, so I felt better watching her drag her feet into the office.

"So?" I whispered to Dezzie, who was still standing in the middle of the room. "How'd it go?" She jumped like I'd yelled "Boo!"

"Fine." She nodded. "I'm not supposed to say anything, though. Just go in there and answer him." She shrugged, and before I could ask her another question, Mrs. Pearl motioned with her late pass and Dezzie left the office, on her way to choir.

My headache and upset stomach had only gotten worse with all the waiting. It seemed as though Saber was in the principal's office four times as long as Dezzie or Mauri, although when I looked at the clock we'd only all been in there for fifteen minutes.

Finally, Saber came out. At that moment I realized the only thing worse than waiting was when the time was up and it was my turn. My stomach flipped like an acrobat and my throat tightened.

"Hamlet Kennedy."

The only times I'd seen Principal Obin were during events like school assemblies or walking through the hall. I saw him angry when a bunch of boys had been "book bowling" in the hall while he walked by. Then he seemed as large as a bear when he roared at the kids to knock it off.

I tried to get off my chair, but it was like Velcro had been attached to my legs. I couldn't move. I tried again, pushing off the sides, and popped up too fast, nearly falling. Sweating already. Eeek!

When I peeked into his office, Principal Obin was sitting behind his desk, hands steepled in front of his face, hiding his mouth. There was a rumor that went around when I was a sixth grader that he had been an assistant coach on an NFL football team, but no one could prove it. The man had no Google history. He looked like he could *play* professional football, though. At over six feet tall, his shadow stretched down the building's hallways when he went by. He was bald too, which made him look more serious and a little mean. When I stepped into the room, he unfolded his hands and pointed at a chair across from the desk.

"Have a seat, Hamlet," he said. His voice rumbled.

It was a good thing there was a chair there, because I was so nervous I was sure I would have collapsed where I stood. He leaned over his desk, which was large and covered by piles of paper.

"Your art teacher tells me that there was some inappropriate language used in her classroom earlier. And that you were a part of it." He stopped. I nodded.

"As you know, we don't tolerate that type of behavior here at Howard Hoffer Junior High. Now, I would like you to tell me what happened in your own words."

I opened my mouth, but all that came out was a squeak. I cleared my throat and tried again.

"It was a misunderstanding, sir," I explained. I'd never used the term "sir" before in my life, but Principal Obin was *definitely* a sir. I did my best to tell him what happened—it didn't take very long—and he listened with a serious expression the whole time.

"And . . . that's really it," I finished. "Ms. Finch-Bean brought us here to see you." I didn't know what else to say.

He sat back in his chair and put his ankle on top of his other knee, like he was considering what I was saying.

"According to other accounts, you had greater involvement than what you described."

His words filled me with cold liquid fear. They had conspired against me. I took a deep breath, trying to get control of myself.

"Those girls are trying to get me in trouble so they

can be closer to my sister," I explained, hoping he would see and understand the truth. "They treat her like she's a doll." I was pretty sure that I said if Saber and Mauri were cheating off Dezzie, we'd all be in a lot more trouble than we were right now.

He steepled his hands again. "I see," he said.

"It's true," I said. "They don't like me looking out for her so much."

"Thank you, Ms. Kennedy," he said. "I'll take the matter up with Ms. Finch-Bean. However, in the future, may I suggest that when one of your peers makes such a flagrant violation of the rules, that you speak up. Silence equals complicity in the act."

I nodded again, worrying all the while that he didn't believe me.

"And, you may want to remember that even though your sister is . . ." He paused for a second. "Even though your sister is *unique*, she still needs to be surrounded by strong role models. Don't let us, or her, down by reducing yourself to such behavior. Or by caving in to others."

Shame, soaked in responsibility, covered me. How was this my fault? I forced a whispery "Yes, sir" from somewhere in my throat and nodded again.

"You're already late for third period," he said. "I suggest you get a late pass from Mrs. Pearl."

"Thank you, sir," I said, and headed to the office. I wasn't sure what was going to happen—I guessed that he could still get my parents involved or I would still be in trouble with Ms. Finch-Bean, but at that moment I didn't care. I just wanted to get out of there.

Once in the hall, however, some kind of post-principal's office meeting trauma set in. My hands started shaking and my face burned. I couldn't believe that he suggested I wasn't a good enough role model for Dezzie. Shouldn't *she*, as the Genius Child, be a role model for *me*?

My eyes burned with angry tears and I let my feet carry me to the girls' room a few halls away. As I made the last turn, around a bank of lockers, I crashed into someone coming the opposite way. My chin made contact with the person's shoulder, and we both bounced backward.

"Sheesh, Hammie. Take it down a notch, okay?"

KC Rails. He seemed flustered.

Not who I wanted to see right then. I swiped at my eyes and cheeks, trying to remove any tear stains and get myself under control. KC, annoying as he is, is no dummy. "Are you okay? Do you want me to take you to the office?" he asked.

Not what I needed him—or anyone, but especially him—to say.

I didn't have to respond. The spray of tears that exploded from my eyes told him everything I didn't. He stepped out of the way, mouth open in shock, and I fled into the bathroom for the third time that year.

Yeah, bad things come in threes.

ꝯ X ꝰ

That night, I barely slept. Mom and Dad were scheduled to come into my English class the next day. There was no way I could hide from them and the utter humiliation they'd bring. Besides, between my "talent" and the trip to the principal's office, I had a lot to cover up. I twisted and turned in my sheets, trying to figure out how to get out of class, but it was no use. Horrific scenarios that would have given Shakespeare nightmares played on a constant loop in my head:

The Scene: *English class, Mom and Dad stand at the front of the room, in full costume, but Dad wearing his "This above all: To thine own self be true" shirt under his cloak.*

Dad: Prudence will act out this scene with another student.

Scans room while Mom jingles bells on her cloak.

Dad: You—over there. You will do.

Points to Carter Teegan.

Me: *(dies inside)*

Or . . .

The Scene: *English class, Mom and Dad stand at the front of the room, in full costume, Dad also wearing his hat with the goofy feather on it.*

Mom: One at a time, I would like you to read a set of lines while I clap out the rhythm of iambic pentameter.

Nirmal Grover raises his hand.

Mom: Yes?

Nirmal: What's "iambic pentameter"?

Mom (gives Mrs. Wimple her patented teacher glare): You do not know? Truly?

Everyone shakes their heads.

Mom: Than I shall introduce you to the wonders of stressed and unstressed syllables!

Me: *(dies inside)*

Or . . .

The Scene: *English class, Mom and Dad stand at the front of the room, in full costume, Dad holding a giant mead flask.*

Mrs. Wimple: Dr. and Dr. Kennedy—Hamlet's parents, for those of you who don't know—

have graciously agreed to let us benefit
from their expertise as we study Shakespeare.

Mom: Thank you, Mrs. Wimple.

Mrs. Wimple: Did I mention that they are
Hamlet Kennedy's parents? Hamlet, who is
sitting over there? *(gestures in my direction)*

Me: *(dies inside)*

When my alarm finally went off, my sheets were as
tangled as my brain. How could Mom and Dad do this
to me, especially after everything else? Why couldn't they
see that they were so strange? Or that normal society had
moved beyond 1650 and that Shakespeare wasn't the
most important thing on the planet?

Weeks of pressure, stress, and hiding had built up to
this. Mom and Dad would process into school like Elizabethan royalty, hear me perform, discover that I'd been
in the principal's office, and learn all the Shakespeare
secrets I'd been hiding from them. My stomach felt like
the carnival balloon animal guy was at work in there.

I dragged myself out of bed and into the shower, my
body feeling like a bag of marbles. The hot, steamy water
cleared my head a little, but once I finished I had to figure
out what to wear.

I finally settled on an outfit and got dressed, and a tap
came at my door.

"Come in," I grumbled. I went to my desk and stuffed my books into my bag.

"Mom says we are going to be late," Dezzie said. She stood just over the threshold, hands bunched at her waist. Her hair was down and she had on a green trapeze shirt and black leggings. "You didn't have breakfast."

Her mention of food made that carnival guy in my stomach create a balloon dog.

"Not hungry," I said. I slung my bag over my shoulder.

"I wasn't either. As a matter of fact, Hamlet, I am rather concerned."

I let my bag slide to the floor. What did *she* have to be concerned about? She wasn't hiding—and as it occurred to me, she said it.

"I don't want them to find out about our visit to Principal Obin's office, and I feel it is inevitable." She rocked back and forth: heel, toe, heel, toe. I flashed back to that first day of school, in front of Mrs. Pearl's desk.

"Me neither," I said. "And I don't know how to prevent that."

Dezzie sighed. "And—Hamlet . . . what if . . ." she squeaked. "What if they discover my artistic failure? The Pollock paintings will be hung all over the school today."

"I don't think they'll be up yet," I answered, trying to soothe her with a lie. Ms. Finch-Bean was planning to hang some today, I was pretty sure. But, really, a bad painting? Even though Dezzie had always done every-

217

thing perfectly, one poor art assignment didn't compare at all to what I had to worry about. "Besides, once they find out that our Globe theaters are going to be judged by 'outside experts' I'm done for. Dad will be so upset that I didn't tell him." I picked my bag up again, then groaned. "And I don't even *want* to know what they have planned for my English class."

Dezzie seemed startled when I mentioned the theater project, probably surprised that I brushed off her issues. I gave her a sympathetic smile to make up for it. She twirled a piece of hair around one finger.

"This could be very bad," she said.

All through Mr. Hoffstedder's history class, I willed time to stop. Usually, his "discussions" were so boring that I'd glance at the clock and only three minutes would have gone by. That morning, it seemed when I blinked ten minutes had passed. Even the discovery of the eighth pig in my locker between classes didn't serve as enough distraction. I simply put him with the others, feeling like we were all wallowing in the same muck.

Art was just as bad. I couldn't focus on my dream journal, and Saber's and Mauri's giggles and chatter with Dezzie didn't help. Time was distorted, like one of Salvador Dalí's paintings.

What seemed like a second later, Dezzie was pushing me out of art and I was contemplating hiding in the girls' bathroom for all of English. The visions of what could happen from the night before popped into my head, and I saw Mrs. Wimple telling everyone over and over again that they were my parents.

As I came down the hall, dragging my feet with each step, Mom's voice cut through my nightmare and brought it to life. I wished I'd made it to the bathroom already.

"Some of them are quite good, but this is truly an example of poorly executed juvenile art if I have ever seen it." I turned my head, and there they were—standing in front of the display of abstract expressionist–inspired pieces that Ms. Finch-Bean had hung outside the main office. And the "poorly executed" painting was Dezzie's. For a second, I felt worse for her than me. At least she wasn't around for the shock of having my parents criticize something she'd done. I coughed, and my mom turned around.

"Honey, there you are! How fortuitous, Roger!"

My dream swapped with reality:

Mom was dressed in her full Ren Faire attire—wine-colored velvet dress, cloak, and kerchief hat. Her hair was pulled into a bun, and she carried a drawstring satchel. I couldn't see what she had on her feet—the skirt was too long—but I was guessing it was Birkenstocks.

Dad was decked out in his tights, with a ruffled shirt and short cloak. At least he wasn't wearing one of the Shakespeare T-shirts.

Wait, that was a *good* thing?

I was so focused on their humiliating attire that for a second I didn't see the other kids who were also frozen in place in the hall, staring. As if anyone in the school needed more proof that we were the freak family.

Plus, there was the stuff that other kids couldn't see, like my imminent reading doom. Or the way Mom and Dad were so wrapped up in Dezzie, yet didn't seem to care about me. Perhaps I could join another Ren-family somewhere.

The bell buzzed, breaking me out of my trance.

"Will you show us the way to your class, m'lady?" Dad said, making a sweeping bow.

I gave him a robot nod and turned my back to them. My face jumped and twitched as I fought against tears. Inhaling as deeply as I could to regain some control, I put one foot in front of the other and made my way to English while staring at the tips of my shoes. Behind me, the soft rustle of heavy fabric rose above the noise of kids going to class, slamming lockers, and scuffing sneakers on the linoleum floor.

But nothing was louder than the snickers and whispers that floated after us. I was sure my parents were oblivious. Gritting my teeth, I walked faster. At the door to Mrs. Wimple's classroom, I stopped short. I couldn't do it. I couldn't go in.

"Hamlet? Is this the room?" Mom stepped next to me, and the sight of her cloak and cap made me cringe. I dropped my eyes to the floor and nodded.

"Doctors Kennedy!" Mrs. Wimple appeared at the door, all smiles and English class exuberance. "Come in! We are so happy to have you!"

I crept in behind them, hoping the flowing fabric would mask me from the rest of the kids. No such luck.

Every action in the classroom changed. Instead of the loud pre-class talking, fooling around, organizing, primping, and standing, there were quiet whispers and murmurs, nudges and pointing. Grins crept across faces, and their eyes danced back and forth from my parents to me.

I slunk into my seat and hoped an earthquake would hit the East Coast.

"Whoa," Ty whispered to me across the aisle. "They went all out for us, huh?"

I could barely nod, but still felt stupidly flustered at his use of "us."

"Take your seats everyone," Mrs. Wimple called, using a louder voice than was necessary. I kept my eyes glued to my desktop. If I couldn't be invisible, I could play the "you can't see me if I don't look at you" game.

Sweat beaded on my neck like condensation on a window. I dropped my hands to my lap, clenching and unclenching fists.

"I would like to introduce you to the doctors Kennedy. They are here today to help us with our reading of *A Midsummer Night's Dream*. I hope you will give them the same courtesy that you give me and each other." Mrs. Wimple finished her introduction and I still didn't look up. I held on to a shred of hope that they wouldn't do anything—

"Lords and ladies, we are pleased to make your acquaintance," Dad said.

—overly weird or Shakespearean.

"How do," Mom said.

How do I get out of this? I wondered. I took deep breaths, trying not to panic, knowing my secret would be let loose soon. Should I try to fake and stumble my way through the reading? Mrs. Wimple wouldn't let me get away with that, I was sure. For distraction, I played mental connect the dots with the faint pencil marks on the surface of the desk.

"We are going to undertake an exploration of the Bard's poetic structure and language," Mom went on.

"How about the structure of that outfit," came a snide whisper to my left. I sank lower in my seat.

"As I was saying," my mother continued, "we are going to talk about the poetic structure and the language of the Bard." While she was speaking, my father took a pile of papers out of a bag I hadn't noticed he was carrying. He passed them out to the first person in each row.

When Julie Kennelly turned around to pass me mine, she grinned. "I totally understand how you got your name," she said. I mumbled something in reply and snatched the handouts from her.

"Reading and Reciting the Bard," was printed at the top. And, underneath it: "You Can't Recite the Bard, So Don't Even Try."

"Shakespeare," my father said, "is meant to be *lived.*"

"Is that why you're dressed like that?" came a voice from the opposite side of the room. I couldn't be sure, but I thought it was Mark Sloughman. My brain and body battled out my desire to flee.

"Actually, yes," said my mother. Then she glared at him over her glasses. "And *you* are impudent and shameless."

Her remark—one that she used a lot at home—broke some of the tension in the room, and everyone laughed. Well, nearly everyone. I was still hoping for a fire drill.

Dad went on to explain how, in order for us to be able to act out the elements in the play, we had to understand what was being said before we said the words. Then we'd be able to put the right emphasis on the syllables. So he and Mom wanted to talk about the play, first.

"Puck is a trickster," Mom said. "He loves to get everything confused and gives people the wrong information for his amusement. Let us look at an example. In act two, scene two, Puck sprinkles his dust into the wrong person's eyes. Who is playing Puck in this production?"

I held my breath. There was no way I was going to volunteer any information.

"You mean you don't *know?*" Mrs. Wimple gasped.

"I am afraid I do not," Mom said. "Who is it?"

Everyone in the room was staring at me. Even though my head was down, I knew it.

"Come, come," my father said. "We are short on time."

"It's Hamlet," Mrs. Wimple said.

"Hamlet?" my mother said, incredulous.

"Of course. I assumed you knew. Hamlet, please read your part."

I opened my mouth, but no sound came out. My parents exchanged confused expressions while they waited.

I tried again. The words were a whisper: "Churl, upon thy eyes I throw/All the power this charm doth owe. When thou wakest, let love forbid/Sleep his seat on thy eyelid."

In spite of my mortification, the words flowed just like they had in my room when I practiced. My parents stood straight and stock-still in their ridiculous attire. If they were punctuation, they would have been exclamation points.

"Lovely work, Hamlet, as usual," Mrs. Wimple said. My mother gave a stiff nod.

"Fascinating," my father murmured. "We had no idea."

I'd hoped it would stay that way. Although now that it was out in the open—strangely!—I felt better. Not great—my parents were still living history in front of my classmates—but better. Whoa.

Mrs. Wimple politely cleared her throat. "Our class time," she began, "is short—"

"Of course. Of course. That is how the Bard is to be expressed," my mother said, recovering. Her eyes slid to me every so often. She went on, talking about the different characters—all the stuff I'd heard in class, and growing up, and from Dezzie when talking to Saber and Mauri. I started to relax. It was like a regular English class—except for the fact that my parents were leading it and my father was wearing tights. Now that my secret was out, I almost started to breathe again.

"Now that we are clear on the meaning of the words, we need to understand how they are supposed to be said," Dad said. "That is where iambic pentameter comes in. The richness of the language is magnified by the syllabic structure. I would like everyone to clap the following rhythm with me." He held up his hands. No one moved. Probably because my mother was holding a tambourine.

"This is how we shall illustrate the stressed and unstressed syllables," my mother said. She shook her tambourine for emphasis and the bells tinkled. "They are as follows: da-DUM da-DUM da-DUM . . ." And she went on, whacking the tambourine with every DUM. Evidently, the lack of interest was not to her liking.

"Stand up!" she ordered. "You wear out thy youth with shapeless idleness!" At her curt tone, everyone—me and Mrs. Wimple included—sprang to our feet.

Mom sure could command a room, I thought, feeling a tiny bit of pride. But it was just a tiny, tiny bit.

"Now," Mom said, her cloak flowing about her in a crimson wave, "you shall feel the words in your marrow."

In spite of my thoughts the moment before, the only thing my marrow was feeling was deadly mortification. I was pretty sure this type of parental involvement torture was illegal in several states—or should be.

"Together, we will march and repeat the lines from act two: Weaving spiders, come not here;/Hence, you long-legg'd spinners, hence!/Beetles black, approach not near;/Worm nor snail, do no offence." She and my dad said they'd show us an example.

"We need a volunteer from the audience." No one raised their hands.

"You, good sir. Would you be so kind as to offer your services to my wife and me?" A titter danced around the room. I didn't want to see who they were accosting, but like driving past a car accident, I had to look.

Carter Teegan.

The expression on his face was one of pure horror.

"Uhh, actually . . ." he said.

"You will participate," Mrs. Wimple snapped. She moved next to his chair and he stepped forward. I wanted to crawl under a rock.

The three of them marched around the room saying the lines, Mom banging on the tambourine in rhythm to the words: Wea-VING [clang!] spi-DERS [clang!] come NOT [clang!] . . . The bells on Mom's cloak providing a lightly tinkling accompaniment, Carter dragging his feet as much as he could, face as red as my mom's costume.

You get the idea.

I dared to sneak a peek at Ty. He looked as horrified as I felt, knowing that we'd be next. Ely wore a smirk, like he wouldn't participate unless someone physically made him. Mrs. Wimple was nearly weeping with joy, she was so excited. She hustled us into a line—giving Ely an extra nudge or two to get him moving—while Mom wrote the verse on the board in her precise handwriting.

I stood between Ty and Ely. A combination of pity for me and embarrassment for themselves radiated off them. I stared at the back of Ty's neck, determined not to look anywhere else. A small glimmer of hope surfaced: After all these years, maybe he'd finally be so embarrassed by my family that he'd stop liking me? Maybe?

"And we are ready!" Dad said, voice at the front of the line brimming with cheer. "Weaving spiders, come not here . . ." We stepped forward and snaked around the room, winding through the rows of desks, muttering the lines. Mom's clanging tambourine and bells attempted to keep us on beat.

By the third lap, we were in sync. The marching, chanting, and ringing bells put me in a state of horrified hypnosis. It was like a Greek myth, where I was doomed to do the same thing over and over again forever—time, I was sure, had stopped.

"Huzzah!" my mother cheered after two more laps. "Success!" We stopped, and I almost crashed into Ty. My near-stumble caused my attention to shift to the rest of the room. The other kids also seemed dazed, but Mrs. Wimple wore a wide smile.

"Did you feel the precision of the words?" Mom said, peering over her glasses at Nirmal. He nodded, clearly afraid that if he said no my mom would take him to the stocks.

"I felt it!" Mrs. Wimple said. Excitement shot off her in beams.

"Do we have time for another exercise, then?" Dad said. Sweat beaded on his forehead. I guess clapping and walking and chanting was more of a workout than he was used to.

"Sadly, no," Mrs. Wimple said. "It's just about time for the bell—" And it buzzed.

I didn't want to face anyone—my parents, Ty, Ely, or Mrs. Wimple—and have to talk about what had just gone on. Without looking, without waiting, I bolted from my place in line, snagged my book bag off the floor, and ran out of the room.

ꜿ X i Ꜿ

I raced through the halls, trying to get as far away from English as possible. I thought about hiding in yet another girls' room, but with the passing period, they'd all be filled.

I found myself at the front of the school, outside of James's office door. I dug in my bag for the pile of Go Cards he'd given me, and wrote my name on all of them. If this wasn't an outright parental emergency, I didn't know what was.

I was just about to slip the stack under his door when it opened.

"Hamlet?" James asked. He had a lunch bag in his hand. I was about to make an excuse, but when I opened my mouth, I just burst into tears.

He pulled me into the room, where I collapsed into one of the big green chairs. This time, letting myself sink into it, I felt comforted. For a few minutes, I just cried—completely embarrassed, but unable to stop. James sat across from me, quiet, handing me tissue after tissue.

229

When I finally slowed down and started to breathe normally, he asked me what was wrong.

And the tears came back.

A few minutes later, we tried again. I told him about everything—the iambic disaster, the unfairness surrounding Dezzie, the mac and cheese—all of it. Okay, all of it except for Ty, the locker mystery, and Carter. I couldn't go there. He just sat there and listened.

When I was all talked out, I flopped back into the chair.

"Feel better?" James asked. I nodded.

"Good. You killed my box of tissues." He held it up, empty, for me to inspect. I gave him a weak smile. "Hamlet, you do realize that you are not crazy, right? That you have every right to feel embarrassed by this stuff?"

I gaped at him. I did?

He smiled. "It doesn't make your parents terrible people," he said. "They just seem a little clueless. They don't see things the way you do. You need to talk to them and explain how you feel, and why you feel that way. That's the only way they can understand you."

"But it's hard," I said. "They don't *hear* me."

"I know," James said. "But I can give you some strategies to use that might help. Do you want to me to do that?"

"Yes, please."

He told me a few things—like using the phrase "I feel angry/upset/embarrassed when you bang tambourines in my English class" and giving specific examples instead of just saying how unfair they were. I let him prattle on, but I knew his tools would *never* work. Not with my parents.

"And, I have to tell you, you should let yourself feel proud of how you read Shakespeare. Not a lot of people can do that," he said.

I wasn't sure if I was ready to feel good about anything that came out of English class yet, so I kind of grunted and changed the subject.

"What about the kids in class?" I asked. "They'll never let me live this down."

He smiled. "It wasn't you up there with the tambourine. And something else will happen that will make them forget. Junior high just works that way."

I wish I could say that made me feel better, but it didn't.

The one thing that James hadn't counted on? It seemed that the kids in my class were just as embarrassed by the whole pentameter parade as I was. No one wanted to bring it up, because we were all held prisoner by the echoes of that clanging tambourine. It was like we, as a group, decided never to speak of it again.

My parents, though, had lots of things to say about my role as Puck and my reading talent—mostly along the lines of "we are so surprised," and "why did you not tell us?" They said they were proud of me too—a lot of blah blah blah praise that they usually gave to Dezzie. For my part,

I wasn't ready to confront them about how embarrassing the whole scene had been. Not when they'd finally said something nice about me. And not when I was still just MAD at everyone. So I just did what I always do: pretended that nothing had happened and tried to forget the whole thing.

My relief only went so far, though, because the other thing I couldn't forget was being called into the principal's office.

The Scene: *Home, three days after the principal incident, two days after the Iambic Disaster. Dezzie, hunched over books, in front of the History Channel; Hamlet hovering in the background.*

Me: Did you tell Principal Obin the truth?

Dezzie (not looking up): Of course.

Me (dying to know what Principal Obin said to her): We could talk about it.

Dezzie: Did *you* tell him the truth?

Me: Yes.

Dezzie (satisfied): Then there's nothing to talk about.

Me (frustrated): What does that mean? Of course there's something to talk about.

Dezzie: It means that he knows what he needs to deal with the situation. It was a misunderstanding.

Me: I'll say. He seemed to think that I had something to do with it.

Dezzie's shoulders stiffen slightly.

Dezzie: Really?

Me (watching closely): You wouldn't have said anything to let him believe that, would you?

Dezzie (not looking up from her textbook): Of course not, Hamlet.

Not exactly the conversation I was hoping for.

For days, I'd been worrying nonstop that Mr. Obin would call our parents or call us in to his office again. But except for Ms. Finch-Bean splitting us up for two periods in art, it seemed that there weren't any consequences to Mauri's outburst. That in itself was frustrating, because I felt like we'd all gotten in trouble for no reason, and the one person who started the whole thing got off easy.

The following week, my nerves had somewhat settled and pig number nine had appeared in my locker: blue with white stripes. I no longer thought Ms. Finch-Bean was going to punish me, and I stopped feeling as though Principal Obin was lurking around corners, waiting to drag me into his office. What didn't go away was the annoyance at being told I wasn't a good enough role model for my sister. It made me short and irritable with her . . . or when anyone else talked about how wonderful she was.

Like Carter Teegan, for example.

"She's so great," he said one day, leaning against his locker talking to Mark. Not that I was eavesdropping or walking by particularly slowly; I just happened to catch his words. Now each time I saw him, all I could think of was "meringue," thanks to Judith. Even though I no longer went weak in the knees when he came by, he *was* still nice to look at.

"It's *math*, dude," Mark responded. "And it's all you ever talk about lately." He twirled his locker combination and stuffed a handful of papers onto an already overflowing shelf. Now I knew where his perpetually missing homework went. "Cool that you understand it, but whatever. You're starting to sound like you like it. Or her—the baby tutor!" He made a face.

"You're the baby," Carter replied. "Look, it's not just me she's helping out. Seriously. Mauri and Saber were sure they'd bomb English until they started hanging with her. And if they got less than a B this term, Mauri's dad wouldn't take them skiing over break. Now they just write down everything she says and ace their work."

So *that's* why Saber and Mauri were interested in Dezzie's brain—a family ski trip?! It was like a magician whipping a sheet off a table and making a rabbit appear. A ridiculous, shallow rabbit. I'd been right about them all along.

Unfortunately, my discovery took place in the middle of a corridor, with people changing classes on all sides. Someone pushed past me, catching me off guard and knocking me into the side of the lockers with a bang. Carter and Mark turned in my direction as I was straightening up and rubbing the spot on my ribs where a bruise was sure to appear later on.

"Hey," said Mark. Carter didn't say anything, just looked through me like I was a window. I was surprised to find that I truly didn't care.

"Should we start calling you Crash instead of Ham?" KC's voice was at my side. A sizzle raced across the back of my neck.

"Hey," I squeaked to Mark, ignoring KC, who'd probably come by to analyze my less-than-graceful moves or poke fun at my locker shelf pig collection. I didn't care what he said or did, though—discovering why Dezzie was being used changed embarrassment to anger.

"Blow-Out Bacon?" KC wasn't going to let this go. I glared at him.

"How about we start calling you 'KC the toad-spotted nut hook' instead," I snapped, resorting to the first insult that came to mind. Unfortunately, it was one that my father used a lot.

The guys stared at me like Shakespeare himself had sprouted from my forehead.

"Maaannn," said Mark with a low whistle. "That's low."

"Toad-spotted nut hook," Carter mumbled, eyes on KC. "I like that."

KC's freckled face broke into a wide smile.

"Nice one," he said, and laughed. "Shakespeare, right?"

How did he know? I smiled too.

"Wicked Willie," offered Mark.

The warning bell buzzed.

I gathered my stuff together and limped back into the flow of crowd traffic, pleased that I'd held my own with the boys and had finally been able give KC the zinger he deserved.

This school year felt as foreign and strange as one of Dalí's landscapes, and my thoughts and emotions were awkward and hard to handle. Part of me felt bad for Dezzie—she thought Saber and Mauri were "real" friends, and when she finally accepted the truth, she'd be so upset. Another part was angry with her—why hadn't she listened to me in the first place? People were going to take advantage of her because of her brains. She needed to protect herself. But then again, Dezzie— or anyone else in my family, for that matter—had no idea how to fit in or what to expect from the real world. And, really, I hadn't realized how bad it could get either. And I *thought* I fit in.

I spent the rest of the morning trying to figure out how to approach Dezzie about it, and glaring at Saber and Mauri whenever I saw them. I picked at my lunch. Ty, ever-observant and always hungry, eyed my PB&J sandwich.

"You gonna to eat that?" he said.

"Go ahead." I pushed the sandwich, still wrapped, across the table to him and pulled my hand back fast so there'd be no chance he could touch it or brush against it "accidentally."

"What's your story?" he asked, then took a huge bite. Crumbs sprinkled onto the tabletop. I fiddled with the straw in my milk carton. "You've been acting weird."

I *felt* weird. I didn't know how to talk to him anymore. I was afraid that anything that came out of my mouth he'd take to mean that I liked him too. But I missed him, and needed him now to help me figure out how to talk to Dezzie. I didn't know where to begin.

"Where're Ely and Judith?" I asked, trying to change the subject.

Ty polished off the other half of my sandwich before answering. "Ely's meeting with James got moved to today, and Judith said she had a dentist appointment when I saw her this morning. So what's the deal?"

There was no way to avoid it. I took a deep breath, and, keeping my eyes on the sticky plastic table, I explained what I'd heard Carter saying in the hall and what I'd figured out. It didn't take long. While I was talking, Ty munched on the apple from my lunch. Things felt almost normal—like they always had—between us. No peacocking, no displays; just me and Ty.

"That's bad news," he said, swallowing a big mouthful. I relaxed. "It's worse than we thought."

I nodded. "I know."

"What do your parents think about it?"

"They believe her, not me."

Ty shook his head. "Hello, clueless. Were they mad that you didn't tell them about Puck?"

I shook my head. "Not really. I haven't talked to them much."

"So what's your next move?" I snatched the cookie that he was trying to steal from my lunch bag.

"I have no idea," I answered, stashing the cookie in my backpack for safety. "Tell Dezzie again, I guess. She probably won't believe me, though."

"Bet you she's going to be ticked when she finally does," he said, stuffing his own cookie into his mouth. I was so upset about so many things, I couldn't even worry if that was a display. The bell rang, signaling the end of the period.

"You have no idea."

ᵔ Xii ᵔ

On my walk home, I turned options for explaining things to Dezzie over and over in my mind. Saber and Mauri were using her, causing her to betray me, and I still had to babysit her feelings. Just like I'd never tell her what my parents said about her painting because she'd be too upset if she knew. With each step I took, I also became more and more annoyed at the situation.

Why was I the one who had to tell her? Did it really matter? It's not like Saber and Mauri were selling their notes online or anything—they were just trying to pass so they could take a stupid family vacation. Couldn't Dezzie just deal with it herself?

But what went on in art made this a whole different situation. They thought they could get me to take the blame for Mauri's mouthiness. That was low. I needed Dezzie to hear me out this time—to be the "role model" that Principal Obin said I should be. Because of anyone in my house, I had the best chance of getting her to listen to me. Mom and Dad were a lost cause.

I came in through the kitchen door—the same way I always did. But things weren't anything like they always were when I got home.

Both of my parents were sitting at the kitchen table. Usually, Mom was home first in the afternoon—Dad taught a later class and stayed to grade papers and sonnets. Usually, Mom was busy in her office when I came in. Instead, both were sitting in silence, staring at me as though they were waiting for the door to open. Iago was at my dad's feet, also looking grumpy. I froze as I stepped inside.

"Close the door, Hamlet," my mother growled. I reached behind me and did what she asked.

My parents shot looks at each other. Were they taking lessons from Saber and Mauri? My father lifted his round glasses and ran a hand over his face.

"Something is very wrong, Hamlet," my mother clipped. "In fact, something is rotten in the state of Denmark, I would say."

So they were angry. With me. That much was clear. But for what? Then it occurred to me: Principal Obin must have gotten around to calling them.

I took a deep breath. "I meant to tell you, but—"

"How could you?" Dad broke in, not even letting me finish. His eyebrows scrunched together behind his glasses.

"It wasn't even *me*," I said. "I was just there when it happened."

"That is not an excuse," Dad went on. "It was your responsibility."

My emotions swirled. "*My* responsibility? I didn't even *say* anything."

Mom must have been really angry, because she didn't even correct my contractions. Tendrils of hair escaped from her bun and floated around her head like man-eating vines.

"Exactly," she said. Her words came out like small pecks. "You have been concealing a great deal from us lately. First Puck, and now this? We were right up here the whole time. You should have gotten one of us *immediately.*"

"But—" I nearly responded, but cut myself off. Something *was* rotten in Denmark. We weren't talking about the same thing. And what did me not telling them about Puck have to do with anything? I thought we were over that. That it wasn't even an issue!

"Wait," I tried again, struggling to calm down. "What's this about?"

"Do you mean, 'What are we speaking of'?" my mother said. "You knew a moment ago!" Dad just shook his head.

"Honestly," I snipped, struggling to stay calm and get to the root of this situation. I scooped Iago off the floor as protection and stroked his fluffy fur. "Listen to me: I don't think we're talking about the same thing."

My mother let out an impatient sigh. My father put his

241

hand over hers, took his glasses off and rubbed his face again. He has much more patience than she does.

"The Globe, Hamlet. *My* Globe."

For a moment, I had no idea what he was talking about. What globe? I tried to figure it out. "Your theater?"

He nodded. Mom sighed again. "Explain to us what happened."

"I don't *know* what happened," I said. "Is there something wrong with it?"

"Quite a bit," my dad said. I could see that he was trying to keep his anger in control, clamping his mouth closed when he was done speaking. At least I had a little more of a clue. "Look." He pointed to the dining room.

I crossed the kitchen and went in.

At first I couldn't see what the problem was. The wooden Globe, the one made out of the house shingles, sat on the dining room table on its plywood base. As I got closer, though, it became obvious: The walls were askew. The stage slanted. Globs of glue dotted the seat cushions. Either the Globe had been the only casualty in the earthquake I'd been wishing for off and on for months, or it'd been dropped and repaired poorly. Dad must have been brokenhearted.

"I haven't seen it since the day Ty and I were downstairs late last month," I said honestly. Ty had taken our theater home to finish working on it. I hadn't even been back in the basement since that day. Iago squirmed in my arms and I put him down.

"Did your friends do something to it? Did it fall?" From behind me, my dad's voice sounded quiet and even, but when I turned around I saw that he was chewing his cheek like it was the biggest piece of bubble gum on the Eastern seaboard.

"No one touched it," I said, annoyed that they would be quick to accuse my friend. "And it didn't fall—it couldn't. It was on the table down there. What happened to it?"

"That is what we are trying to find *out*," my mother snapped, finally getting involved with the conversation again. "Obviously, nothing could happen to it by itself, and clearly Desdemona would not have touched it."

Desdemona would not have touched it??? That *stung.* Of course Dezzie would never do anything wrong, never mess up someone's project. It was like since she was smart, she *had* to be good too. Such things were beneath her intellect. Even though I knew it was a bad idea, I couldn't stop my brain from saying what came next. All of James's "strategies" for talking to my parents were buried under the rubble of anger and unfairness.

"She's not perfect, you know. Even though you act like she is."

"This is not about your sister," my father said. "It is about the theater."

"But it *is* about her—because you automatically assumed it was *me* who wrecked it!" I wrestled with the anger that bubbled up inside me.

"You were using it last," my father pointed out.

That magician's shallow rabbit appeared on the table in my mind.

"But I wasn't. Saber and Mauri came over after school. Dezzie took them to the basement when she showed them the house," I said.

"I have not seen them," Mom said, eyes narrowed. "How could they come here without me knowing?"

The day came flooding back to me. "You weren't here," I recalled, speaking quickly. "It was the day you had a faculty meeting." I explained the situation as I remembered it. And while I was telling them the story, I remembered something else: I'd heard Saber and Mauri go back downstairs without Dezzie when Saber's mom came to pick them up.

"You know you are not allowed to have anyone to the house when we are not home unless it is Ty," my mother said, sounding shocked. "It is against the rules."

"*I* didn't have anyone to the house," I pointed out. "Dezzie did!"

"She would never break the rules so flagrantly," my mother said.

"Obviously, she did," I responded, furious. "And she didn't tell you about it either. Why do you always think she's so perfect? She's *not.* And that 'poorly executed, juvenile' painting you saw at school was *hers!*" I yelled the last part, because I'd pushed back from the table.

Dezzie stood at the top of the stairs, frozen, and shock

244

displayed all over her face. I hoped she heard what I said. Served her right. I was sick of trying to protect her and hurting myself in the process.

I stormed past her, into to my room, slammed the door, and threw myself across the bed.

I lay there and fumed. I couldn't talk to my parents, because They. Just. Didn't. Listen. The anger was back. I popped off the bed and paced across the floor, not knowing what to do with my energy.

A while later, when I'd somewhat calmed down, I stopped pacing and sat down on the bed again. I heard a tapping at the door.

"Go away." I figured it was Dezzie, finally wanting to talk about everything.

"Honey, open up." Dad's voice came through. "We want to talk to you."

I didn't say anything.

"Please," Mom said. "We want to listen."

If she hadn't said that, I wouldn't have let them in.

"Fine," I muttered into my pillow. The door swung open. Mom and Dad stood there, heads low, hands twisting.

"We owe you an apology," Mom said. "May we come in?"

I nodded curtly. They entered and each perched on my bed. I didn't move or make room for them.

"We do not think Desdemona is perfect, Hamlet. No one is," Dad began. He fiddled with his glasses.

"You know what I mean. Just because she's so smart, you let her get away with all kinds of things—or make me do things for her." My anger sizzled.

Both Mom's and Dad's expressions were complete blanks. I went on. "Like skipping my classes in the afternoon that time to walk her home, or asking *her* all about *her* work and making me run around the school to take her to her classes when she knows her way, and I'm late and missing lunch and algebra—which I'm *failing*, by the way!" Tears flowed down my cheeks and dripped onto the quilt.

"Honey, we're just trying to look out for her," my mother said, breaking her own grammar rule for once. She reached across the bed and put a hand on mine. I snatched it away.

"Then why are you making *me* do it?"

"Because we have more confidence in you," my father said simply. His words nearly knocked me to the floor.

"You *what?*" I asked.

"You're older, you have better decision-making skills, and you have more experience in the world than she," my dad said, ticking the reasons off on his fingers. "We trust you to be able to handle life in a way that she cannot." My mother nodded.

"I can see now that we were expecting just as much out of you as we were out of your sister, but in a different way."

I wanted a video camera to capture this conversation. I didn't think I trusted my own ears.

"You ask me to do this stuff because you trust *me* more than *her?*" I asked, wanting to make sure I understood them properly.

They both nodded. "Hamlet, you don't need us to point out that our family situation is a bit . . . unusual," my dad said. His words set off an avalanche of emotion in me. Tears filled my eyes again, but hurt and anger competed with the sadness.

"No one else has parents who wear cloaks and bells, or a sister who can do calculus but isn't tall enough to reach the bathroom sink!" I blurted. "It's *hard!*"

They glanced back and forth at each other and Mom wrung her hands. "I had no idea you felt that way, honey," Mom said.

"Because you don't pay any *attention,*" I cried. I brushed the tears away angrily. "You're so wrapped up in your Shakespearience that you don't see anything except what you want to see. Most people don't live and act like you. Most parents don't come to school dressed in costume and banging *tambourines!*" My voice was screechy and I needed to blow my nose. I settled for blotting it with the edge of my sleeve and took deep, shuddery breaths.

"We made a choice to follow our passion," Dad said, eyes soft and gentle behind his glasses, "in hopes that you and your sister would follow yours."

Now I felt even more horrible, like I was crushing my parents' dream by spilling my ever-twisting guts. I blotted again.

"I see," I said, even though I didn't. "It's just that your passion leaks into everything in my life too, and it's not the same passion I have. I just want to get through eighth grade."

Dad sighed. "Believe it or not, we value that in you, Hamlet. You are the best-equipped person to help Desdemona—and, in some cases, your mother and me—navigate the world outside of our home. It's not easy for her."

"And we can see now that it has not been easy for you either," Mom said.

"But you've done so well with your responsibility, that we truthfully hadn't even given it a second thought," Dad said, a rueful smile on his face. "We were wrong. And we appreciate all you've done for your sister and us. And we should have paid more attention to the effect it had on you."

Warmth flooded me at his words. The tears didn't stop, but they changed from the streams of hurt to droplets of relief.

"And we will speak with your sister about the damage done to the theater and about obeying the rules of the house," my mother finished.

Tentative hope bloomed in my chest. Maybe they could change. Maybe *we* could change.

Later that evening, my parents had a strict talking-to with their second child, the genius. I tried to listen from my bedroom, but their words were muffled, so I moved to the landing. A tingle of excitement buzzed at the edges of my emotions—I'd never seen my parents upset with my sister—but guilt overrode it. Even though I hadn't been downstairs with Saber and Mauri, while Dezzie and Saber's mom waited, I still felt responsible for what happened to my dad's theater.

The overwhelming feeling, however, was fury.

Saber and Mauri must have thought that the theater belonged to me and Ty and were trying to sabotage our project. How could they do that, just for a ski trip? Obviously I'd know it was them who broke it.

And why hadn't Dezzie said anything to me about it? Why hide it? And why had she continued to be nice to Saber and Mauri after it happened? For that matter, why had she continued to be nice to the destructo twins after what they pulled with Principal Obin?

The tight hum of voices from the kitchen subsided. I scooted back to my room and tossed homework papers across my bed to make it look like I'd been busy and not eavesdropping. A light tap came at the door.

Dezzie peeked her head in when I said she could enter. Her gray eyes were cloudy and sad, and the corners of her mouth turned down like they were too heavy to hold up. She carried Iago into my room.

"I got in trouble," she said. I nodded. She climbed onto my bed. Iago sniffed at the sheets. Satisfied this time, he flopped onto my pillow with a sigh.

"It's the first time," she went on. I shrugged.

"Lots of people get in trouble," I said. "It's no big deal. They won't stay mad at you forever."

"I know." She sighed, then glanced up at me with a sparkle to her eyes. "It was kind of fun," she said. "I didn't know what to expect. They even grounded me."

"You are so weird," I said, and laughed at her surprised expression. She smiled too.

"They also were very supportive about my painting, and apologized for viciously criticizing it."

"I'm sorry I told them. And that you heard."

"You were angry," Dezzie said simply. "And it's probably better that they knew anyway." She was quiet for a minute. "It was nice to hear that they do not expect perfection, though. It is unachievable, and sometimes I forget that.

"But I have a bigger problem than our parents," she said. I waited. "Saber and Mauri. I thought they were my friends. I couldn't believe that they'd do something to intentionally hurt you." She picked at a miniscule spot on my comforter, not meeting my eyes. Iago started snoring.

"I don't know, Dez. Maybe it *was* an accident. Or because they're mean, or jealous, or for a hundred other reasons we don't know about."

"Maybe," she said.

"Why didn't you tell me they broke the theater?"

She sighed. "Because I wanted to fix it myself," she

said. "And I didn't want you to think that they were trying to wreck your project. Dad is so scattered, I didn't think he'd notice. But I'm not very good with glue. Or art in general."

She needed to know the rest of the story.

"You have to believe me, Dezzie. They're not your friends."

She kept her eyes on the floor. "I think I've known that for a while, but I wanted you to be wrong," she said. "Even though that's not logical."

"It's how you felt. And feelings don't always make sense. That's why they're feelings—not thinkings," I said, hoping she'd smile. Instead, she cocked her head and considered it.

"Wise words, Hamlet."

I told her what I'd heard earlier that day, and what I thought Saber and Mauri had been up to. The dark clouds filled her eyes as I spoke, but these clouds were bringing a big, dangerous storm.

"So *that's* all they wanted," she said, scowling. "I don't know why I'm so surprised. In my experience, many students are inherently lazy."

"I have to know," I said slowly, "what went on with Principal Obin."

She looked at me, an earnest expression on her face. "I told the truth, Hamlet—that Mauri said it to you. Mauri wanted me to say that you said it to Saber, but I wouldn't do it. I should have realized then that they were using me."

Whew. So I guess he *had* believed us.

"I'm sorry, Dez," I said. "I know you wanted them to be your friends."

"And they were good at pretending they were," she said. She became quiet and scratched at my comforter some more. Iago twitched, dreaming of his glory days as a show dog, I'm sure.

"That's it!" I said.

"What?"

"The pretending. If they could fake being your friend, there's no reason why you can't fake being theirs."

Dezzie shook her head. "But I don't *want* to be friends with them."

"Do you think they should get away with this with no consequences?"

"Not exactly," she said. "But all they want from me is . . ." She trailed off, then started nodding her head.

"You're getting it, aren't you?" I said, and gave her a big grin.

"I think so," she said. "And if you're thinking what I'm thinking, this is going to be good."

"Huzzah!" I cheered.

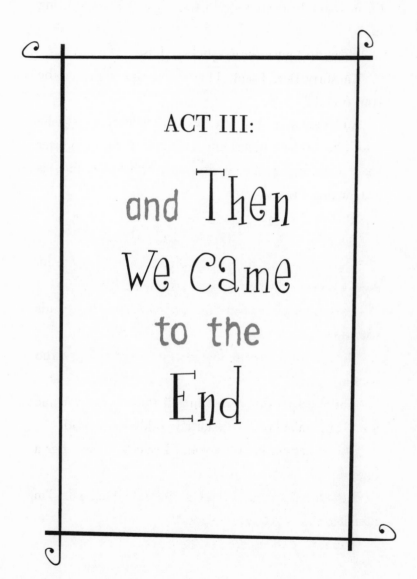

ACT III:

and Then
We Came
to the
End

e need to teach them a lesson," Dezzie declared. She was all business. She flopped onto my pillows, waking Iago, and rolled and unrolled the hem of her Scooby-Doo pajama pants. "They can't cheat off me."

"I agree," I said. "I think I have a plan to make sure that they won't ever do it again." As I explained my idea, Dezzie listened carefully. The plan was simple: Make them sink themselves while we watched. But the longer I spoke, the deeper her eyebrows furrowed.

"Are you sure we can make it work without getting caught?"

"I'll need your help," I explained. "Otherwise, no. And there are a couple more things I need to figure out. Will you do it?"

She flipped onto her stomach, knees bent, feet in the air. The legs of her pajamas slipped down to reveal the trim of her $E=mc^2$ socks. She always wore them before a big test.

"It's diabolical," she said. "I've never done anything so devious."

"But will you do it?" I asked. After what Saber and Mauri had put us through—everyone in my family, including my dad—I wanted nothing more than to create an end to this whole thing that would be, well, Shakespearean.

"Oh, I'll do it," said Dezzie. The furrows were gone, replaced by a smooth forehead and a wide smile. "And it will be epic."

And so was the mountain of pre-algebra homework that I pulled out when she left. One week till the big test. I could only hope *that* ending would be as satisfactory as the one I was concocting.

At school, preparations were in full swing for our Salute to Shakespeare extravaganza. Mr. Hoffstedder reminded us to finish our Globe theaters.

"There's a lot at stake, people," he said. "Remember—your work will be judged!"

I really didn't want to win any Shakespeare prizes.

Ty felt differently.

"We could totally win if your dad told us what to do," he said to me at lunch after Mr. Hoffstedder's announcement. "I could bring it back to your house."

"I don't think that's a good idea," I said.

"It'd be great. He could check it out and we could go to the Spoon after." Judith, who'd been deep in conversation with Ely over something that had happened in her

French class the day before, gave me a pointed look. My heart locked up and my appetite shriveled.

"Uhhh, I don't think so," I said. "That wouldn't be a good idea."

"Didn't you just say that?" Ty asked. He knocked on my forehead. "Something in there stuck on repeat?"

I jerked back from his hand. "Nope. Everything's fine," I said, trying to calm my breathing. Where had that nice, relaxed feeling that I'd had with Ty gone? I plopped my backpack onto the table, digging through it for some imaginary piece of paper to avoid looking at Ty. "We're basically done. And with the whole busted Globe thing, I think it might upset my dad." The excuse sounded lame even to me. Ty turned away, hurt.

As I was trying to figure out what to do next, a piece of paper fluttered out of one of the pockets and into my lap. Another smiling origami pig. Number ten, made from Christmas wrapping paper. I smiled back at it. When I looked up at our group, Ty was scowling.

"What's that?" he said.

"Nothing." I stuffed the pig into the pocket of my jeans. "Just a pig." Ty didn't recognize it? Whew!

"I can only imagine who'd leave you paper swine," muttered Ty. Judith raised an eyebrow at me.

I swept my half-eaten lunch into my bag and pushed my chair back. I had to get away from there.

"Where're you going?" Ely asked.

"I left something in my locker," I said, searching for an excuse. I didn't look at Ty at all, just turned and left. The rest of lunch I lurked in the library, waiting for the bell, analyzing every second of the scene at the table over and over again. Worrying about his every word, being careful about what I said, was wearing on me: I was stressed out and it was ruining our friendship. Since avoiding wasn't working, I was left with only one option: confrontation.

All through my afternoon classes, I couldn't get the Ty situation out of my mind.

"What's bothering you?" Judith asked when I met her after her French class. We started walking to science.

"Two guesses."

"Hamlet, you *have* to talk to him!" she said. "Even if it's just for my and Ely's sake—it's getting hard to be around the two of you."

The two of them?! What about me?

"I know," I said, deciding not to respond to her comment. "But every time I say something, I'm worried that it's the wrong thing or that it won't come out right or he'll think it means something different than what it actually does. And it doesn't." We'd reached the science room.

"Dude, you can't hide from it forever," Judith said.

"Wise words, Judith." I sighed.

That week, in language arts, Mrs. Wimple had us practicing our parts and staging the scenes we were going to perform. All the reading and rereading my classmates were doing was helping their pronunciation, but I would still sound like a native Elizabethan speaker compared to them—that is, if I didn't fall off the stage or freak out when I saw the audience. Just because I could perform in class didn't mean I could perform onstage. But I'd finally realized that there really wasn't anything I could—or should—do about that, so I memorized the lines for Puck and waited for the inevitable. Some of them, I was surprised to find, were fun to say . . . especially the end:

"If we shadows have offended,/Think but this and all is mended./That you have but slumber'd here/while these visions did appear./And this weak and idle theme,/ No more yielding but a dream."

"You are going to shine," Mrs. Wimple said one day as I sat backstage, muttering the lines to myself.

Nirmal Grover, nearby, nodded. "You're so good at this, Hamlet."

His praise surprised me. Soon I'd be another Kennedy who stood out from the crowd. But, I reminded myself, it worked for my mom, dad, and Dezzie. Maybe it would for me too?

Dezzie kept up the façade of friendship with Mauri and Saber better than I expected. Since they'd had "such insight" into *Midsummer*, Mrs. Wimple picked them to give an overview of Shakespeare's life at the beginning of the play. They quizzed Dezzie about his biography every day in art. She answered all of their questions in great detail, and even helped them edit their introduction one day at lunch. Based on the slight smile at the corners of her mouth, she enjoyed the switch from being child genius to child evil genius. There wasn't a cloud to be seen in her eyes.

"You're so good at this," Mauri gushed one day in art class. "I don't know how you remember all this stuff."

Dezzie shrugged. "Some things come easy for me, I guess," she answered. Even her frustration with art seemed to have lessened. She'd actually enjoyed the surrealist dream-journal assignment. Recently, Ms. Finch-Bean gave us the assignment of doing pop art replicas, and Dezzie was working on a series of prints of hydrogen molecules in neon colors.

"Yeah," Saber continued. "It's been so great having you help us."

"I'm just glad to do it," Dezzie said. She snuck a glance at me around her paper. "Anything to help a friend."

We both smiled at that one.

11

The night before the Salute to Shakespeare, my mother came into my room while I was running over my lines one last time. I knew them by heart, but once I was done reviewing them I needed to study for the pre-algebra test. Both options were about as appealing as Mom's poume d'oranges dinner.

"Need some help?" she asked, glancing at the script scattered across my bed.

"I think I have it," I said. I yawned and made room for her to join me. She perched on the edge. "It's a pretty easy scene."

"Not for Puck," she said. Ever since the discussion in my room, Mom and Dad had been much better about asking what I was doing in classes, instead of just focusing on Dezzie. Although it was a little annoying at times—like every night at dessert when they asked me what I'd discussed in my courses that day—I had to admit I liked it . . . even if I didn't tell them about everything. Like the pre-al test that was waiting for me tomorrow. I didn't need them stressing me out even more.

"I guess. It *is* a lot of lines."

"He's a trickster, you know, and one of my favorite characters. Always skirting Oberon to get what he wants and cause trouble."

I nodded. "It seems like he wants to mess stuff up on purpose."

"He thinks that's funny," Mom went on. She smoothed an invisible wrinkle on my comforter. "Some people thrive on others' anxiety."

"I guess so." I thought about the anxiety that eighth grade had caused me so far. Did I thrive on it? Nope. I definitely wasn't the Puck type.

"You've had your fair share of anxious moments recently, I'd wager," Mom said. "This has been a challenging year for all of us."

"Some of us more than others," I said.

"I know, honey. But your dad said it best—we chose to follow our passions. And for the pain that's caused you, I am truly sorry." She patted my knee. "We don't want you to feel badly, or be embarrassed by us. But this is who we are."

"I know." I paused, letting her words sink in. "But what about who I am? Don't you care that I'm not as smart or special as Dezzie?"

My mom's expression turned to one of shock.

"Honey, you are just as special as she is, in our eyes," she answered. "And I'm so sorry that you ever felt any differently."

Her words wrapped around me like a warm blanket. I was quiet for a moment, and then it occurred to me. "What happened to 'commoner's speech'?" I asked, noticing all her contractions.

"I've decided that it's okay to be common sometimes," Mom admitted. "I don't have to be all Shakespeare all the time. I'll try to be a little more 'with it' from now on. Okay? And you have permission to tell me if I'm not."

Finally! Although they'd never be normal parents, maybe they'd try a little harder to be less bizarre. Was that a flicker of hope that I felt?

"But back to Puck, Miss Player," Mom said, shifting gears from our mother-daughter moment. "There's no other character quite like Puck in any Shakespeare play. He messes around with the other players, confusing everyone and getting all of the couples mixed up. His playfulness and lighthearted attitude make him unique, especially in the context of the story."

"Sometimes being unique isn't so great," I said before I could call the words back.

Now it was Mom's turn to be quiet for a minute.

"It's hard to be your own person," she agreed, "especially when those around you are very distinctive. The important thing is for you to carve out your own space in the world. Maybe not as distinctively as Puck, but you can still be unique."

I chewed on that for a few minutes. I'd spent so much

time avoiding being unique that I didn't know where to begin. "Can you maybe help me with that?" I asked, shyness taking over. Even though I'd been given help this year, asking for it—especially from my mom—was hard and foreign.

"Of course!" She brought her fists to her chest in her trademark gesture of excitement. "Let's run through some lines."

Together, we went through my scene. She gave me some pointers on how to tell when Puck was making a sneaky joke, or how to identify when he was trying to act responsible to Oberon. Even though I had no problem *saying* the words, with her help I really understood why I was saying them. Puck was coming to life. Through *me*!

"I brought you something for tomorrow," she said when we were done, gesturing to the wrapped bundle at the foot of the bed. "Maybe it will make you feel more Puck-like."

We were supposed to bring in a costume element that would help us "illustrate our character." Visions of brocade and wide collars spun through my head, weakening the bond we'd just forged.

"You didn't have to," I began, wondering how I could say no without hurting her feelings. She was making an effort, after all.

She handed me the package. The bundle chimed when I lifted it, was soft and not too heavy, wrapped in purple tissue and tied with a silver thread. I took a deep breath, then slid the thread off and unfolded the paper.

Inside was a sheer purple scarf edged with bells. They tinkled lightly, not in an obnoxious way, and it was so delicate it looked as though fairies themselves had made it.

"It's beautiful," I said. And it was—not over-the-top Elizabethan scary, not lame dug-out-of-Grandma's-closet desperate.

"You like it?" Mom asked. Her forehead was creased in a tense line of worry. "I was afraid you'd think it was too distinctive."

"It's perfect," I said. "It's . . . me." I wrapped my arms around her in a big hug.

"That's what I wanted to hear," she said, and squeezed me back.

The next morning, I waited for Ty and his mom outside the main entrance to HoHo. He had the job of transporting our Globe Theatre to school—new promises aside, it probably wouldn't have survived my mother's driving. Around me, other eighth graders were navigating the crowds, carrying all permutations of the theater to the caf, which doubled as an auditorium. Some were made from Popsicle sticks, some from cardboard and construction paper, and even one made from what appeared to be an old hatbox. Ty's mom's car pulled up, and she got out, waving.

"Hi honey," she said.

"Hi, Mrs. Spencer." She knows better than to try to kiss or hug her kid's friends in front of the school . . . a lesson that my mom finally seemed to be learning. Instead, she gave me a big smile. I smiled back.

Together, we slid our balsa wood creation from the backseat. Ty had done a great job painting the seats and backdrop; all we had left to do was set the stage for our scene. I had the characters cut and mounted from Dad's old book in my bag.

"Good luck, you two," Mrs. Spencer said when she saw we had it under control.

"I always think you look funny without your skate-board," I said, trying to figure out something to talk about that wouldn't lead to the confrontation that needed to happen. A little more avoidance couldn't hurt, could it?

We wove through the halls, avoiding clueless sixth graders and curious seventh graders. He'd had to leave the board in the car in order to help carry our project in.

"What's that supposed to mean?" he said.

"Like you're missing something," I explained, all of a sudden realizing that this probably wasn't the best con-versational course. "I'm used to seeing you with it."

He sighed. "I feel naked without it, actually."

"Good thing you're not," Ely said, saving me from more awkwardness as he emerged from the crowd around the caf door. "That'd be a dress code demerit." We laughed—

maybe I laughed a little too hard—and Ely helped us find the numbered table where our theater was supposed to go. The bell buzzed.

"I've gotta go," I said, checking my watch.

"We're excused from homeroom, you know," Ty said, following me to the door. "We're supposed to get the chairs set up in the auditorium and stuff."

"Pre-al re-test," I said, huffing as I picked up speed. "The one I bombed? Mr. Symphony said we could take it early if we were in the play." I gave a quick wave to Ely as I left the gym, relieved.

I slid in the door of Mr. Symphony's first-period class just as the late bell buzzed. Three other people from my class were there, also waiting for the test. KC, Carter, and Chrissy all stood at the back of the room. I scooted farther in to be near them. Hopefully there'd be some strength in numbers, or something. Ha-ha.

"Miss Kennedy." Mr. Symphony nodded in my direction. He then started his class on some word problems so he could get us our tests, and brought the sheaf of paper over to us.

"You four will take this in TLC," he said. "It covers the same concepts as the one you didn't pass, but doesn't feature the same problems—or answers," he said, sending a dark scowl in our direction.

"Gotcha, Mr. S.," KC replied. He held his hand out for

the test pile. Mr. Symphony looked at it, then turned to me.

"*You* may take them, Miss Kennedy," he said. "Tell the TLC staff to return them to me when you're done."

"Yes, sir," I replied, taking the tests from him. "Thank you."

He gave us a curt nod and sent us out.

"Let's see it, Puck," KC said as we walked down the hall.

"No way," I said. "Why do you want to preview a math test for?" KC tried to snatch it out of my hand, but I dodged him.

"Stop it, KC," Chrissy said. "Leave it alone or we'll get in trouble." Carter didn't say anything. It occurred to me then: Carter wasn't a meringue—he was like chicken. Something safe. Something predictable. Something that didn't stand out . . . kind of like the person I'd spent my whole life up until now trying to be.

KC bobbed and weaved around me like a duck on a pond until we got to the TLC room—more funny than annoying for once. When we arrived, Ms. Grafton sent us to separate tables to work.

This time, when I looked at the test, the letters and numbers made sense to me. I recognized the types of problems and the steps I needed to solve them. Not that it was easy— it wasn't—but I didn't feel as though it was written in a language that I'd never seen. I worked my way through, one at a time, using the tools Ms. Grafton taught us during our tutoring sessions. There were twenty problems on the test. I finished all of them and had time to check my work. When I turned my paper in, I smiled at her.

"Nice feeling, isn't it?" she said. I agreed.

Even nicer? I did it on my own, without help from Dezzie. As I was leaving, KC was finishing. He gave me a thumbs-up and a big freckly grin. I grinned back.

"Wait for me," he mouthed. I surprised myself by nodding at him.

In the hall, I regretted my choice. Why had I told KC I'd wait? He'd probably tease me about the upcoming play. Like I needed my nerves rattled now, when I felt so good about what I'd just done.

I wandered around down the hall a little ways, and found that Ms. Finch-Bean had hung our surrealist projects too. It took me a few seconds to find Dezzie's because it looked like the others: funky animals, weird symbols, and vibrant colors. She'd been able to fit in a little, after all.

After going through the row of drawings, I'd nearly talked myself into leaving. Then the door opened.

"You stuck around," KC said.

"Don't sound so surprised," I snapped. I turned toward the stairwell. "I just wasn't in a hurry to set up chairs."

KC skittered behind me. "Why're you so grouchy all the time, Bits?"

"Because you're *annoying*," I pointed out, as if he didn't know the obvious. I went down the stairs. "Do I want to know what Bits is?"

KC slid on the rail next to me. "Bacon Bits."

My insides tightened. "You should get off the railing," I said through clenched teeth. Waiting for him was definitely a bad idea.

"And you need to lighten up," KC said, sliding to the very end. He jumped off and his sneakers made a soft slap on the floor.

"I'm thinking about the play," I said. I pointed out that I had to *perform*. In front of an *audience*. My heartbeat thrummed.

"From what I've heard, you don't have to worry," he said. "You're a great Puck."

I raised an eyebrow at him, but the compliment made me feel good.

"And besides, I wasn't teasing you about the play. Just your name." He jumped up, taking a swipe at a banner advertising the Salute to Shakespeare hanging from the ceiling.

"I know." My face flushed. Why didn't he get why that was an issue?

"I'll tell you a secret," he said. He was making me all jittery inside. Did I want to know his secrets?

Maybe I did.

"It's Kelley," he said.

"Huh?"

"The C's for Christopher. But the K, it's for Kelley."

"That's a girl's name," I said. KC just stared at me.

"Oh!" I cried, and blushed. I tried to recover. "That's not so bad."

"Of course not—it's not yours. That's the point. Some people worry too much about what other people think of them, and need to have more fun—like in the play." He ran one hand across the front of the lockers that we were passing.

"The play is *not* fun."

"But it can be," he said. "You could have fun acting."

"People will say stuff if I mess up," I said. "Or if I do too good a job."

"Most people are lame-os. That's why you have to have fun."

"Most people are," I agreed, thinking of Saber and Mauri. My irritation faded a tiny bit. We were at the door to the caf.

"So Bits isn't so bad?" he asked, his face scrunched into a goofy grin.

"Not so bad," I admitted, "especially considering everything else you've called me."

"Bits it is," he said. "Oh—and you forgot something." He held out his hand.

"I did?"

He leaned over, and, in a flash, slipped a folded paper

into my palm and planted a kiss on my cheek. Before I could even register it, he was gone.

KC kissed me!

It tingled. A smile spread across my face.

And in my hand was an origami pig.

Eeeeee!

⁙ 111 ~

In the caf, chairs had already been put out, and the plastic tables tucked away, but nothing would get rid of the greasy fried lunch smell. At least there was no mac and cheese on the menu today. Thinking back to that day almost made me laugh. Almost.

I wandered around, looking for something to do, but everything seemed to be taken care of. Ty, who had begged Mrs. Wimple to do lights instead of play Theseus—and who got his way—was wedged into a booth in the back of the room staring at switches and dials. I was sick of avoiding things and tired of trying to figure out what he did or didn't mean. Plus, now that things had . . . *changed* with KC, I needed to talk to him.

It was now or never.

I hovered at the edge of the lighting setup—a flat rectangular panel with levers, dials, and switches labeled with pieces of masking tape.

"Hey," he said, eyes down.

"Hey." I bit my lip. "That stuff looks pretty complicated." Ty slid a lever up the board and a spotlight glowed on the other side of the room. "Not really, if you know what you're doing."

"Uhhh, look," I said, not really sure where to begin. "I've been acting strange lately. Stranger than usual. I'm sorry."

"Yeah, you've been *very* strange." His bangs hung in front of his forehead. I couldn't see his eyes, which made it a little easier to speak.

"It's just . . . we're friends, right?" My heart pounded and my throat went dry.

"I thought so." Ty shrugged.

"Well, being friends is important to me. Friends with you, I mean." I sounded like an idiot.

"Okaaay," Ty said. He brushed his hair back and finally met my gaze. "What's going on, Hamlet? Just say it—I have stuff to do."

His directness surprised me so much, I just blurted it out without thinking.

"I don't like you," I said. "I mean, I do, but not in that way." My stomach quivered and I hoped I wasn't going to yurk on the light board.

"You don't *like* me?" Ty said, looking just as surprised as I felt. "You mean, *like* me, like me?"

I nodded and hoped that the ceiling would fall on my head and end this exchange. Shock was not the reaction that I expected—okay, I had no idea what to expect—but this was not it.

"No offense, but I'm glad. That'd be kind of gross." He laughed.

"Yeah, it would be," I said, getting irritated at Ty's amusement with the situation. I'd been worried about this for over a month and he thought it was *funny*? "So why do *you* like *me*?" I crossed my arms.

I'd read about it, but never actually seen someone's jaw drop until just then. His mouth literally fell open.

"I *don't* like you," he said. "Where'd you get that idea?"

At the same time, we both said it: "Judith."

Ty shook his head. "I *told* her not to say anything to you!"

"That's what made her think that you did," I said. Now I felt dumb.

"It was KC," he explained. He'd heard that KC liked me? "But he's such a jerk to you all the time, I figured you'd freak out if you knew."

"And?" I prompted, knowing that there had to be more to Ty's grouchy behavior.

"And I was kind of afraid that if things changed, maybe you wouldn't want to hang out anymore," he confessed. "Especially after I saw how much fun you were having with him in the hall that day a few weeks ago. You hadn't been that comfortable with me in a while."

I flashed back to the day Ty saw me with KC, then all of awkwardness when we were building the Globe and at the Chilly Spoon. No wonder he was upset. "I'll always want to hang out with you," I told him. "And I kind of figured the KC part out." I thought of the origami pigs and the nicknames, then the kiss, and my cheek warmed again.

Remembering it made my insides tinkle like the bells on my purple scarf. "Uh, I'm not so freaked out by it."

"Really?" Ty raised an eyebrow at me.

"Welllll," I said. "Shakespeare would say, 'There are more things in heaven and earth.'"

Ty watched me for a second, and must have realized that I wasn't going to say anything else. "So what do we tell Judith?" he said instead.

"Nothing." I smiled. "We just call her Puck."

Mrs. Wimple started waving her arms and yelling that we had fifteen minutes to get ready for the start of the show. I smiled at Ty, relieved that we could still be who we always were together. I'd spent so much time worried about how things would change, I hadn't seen how much they had changed by me avoiding him. Lame!

Feeling better, I went to find a quiet corner and pulled out my script. This wasn't like when I tried softball, or weaving, or even flying under the radar—this was a new Hamlet: front, center, onstage—a main character. I paced back and forth, reading and rereading my lines. It was

Shakespeare—who I tried all my life to avoid—and I *liked* *it*. And I would be good at it. And everyone would be watching.

Across the room from me came familiar high-pitched giggles. Saber and Mauri were hunched over a notebook, their script scattered on the floor, not paying attention to their parts or anyone else. Carter approached them. His green eyes and blond hair held no magic for me anymore—next to KC's freckles and energy, Carter seemed kind of dim.

They were too far away for me to hear what they were saying, but when Saber showed him their notebook, even I could tell they were playing hangman.

A small shape caught the corner of my eye. Dezzie had come into the room, and from where she was she could also see their game. She saw me looking her way and nodded, a wide smile spreading across her face. Then she tugged at the collar of the tunic she was wearing, revealing the trim of a T-shirt underneath. What was *that* about?

What seemed like seconds later, Mrs. Wimple wooshed us backstage. I added the scarf to my outfit of jeans and a dark blue T-shirt, and gave the bells a tinkle. They chimed softly in the din. My nerves jumped about eight notches higher. I paced around, then peered between the curtains to see the auditorium filling up.

Dezzie was in the front row. There were two seventh-grade language arts classes, Principal Obin, and several teachers—including Mr. Symphony—and a group of older kids I didn't recognize. They seemed too old to be high schoolers, and I couldn't figure out why they'd be there anyway. It seemed like a lot of people. I was sure this was my parents' doing. Why couldn't it just be what it was—a junior high play? My stomach bunched like the stage curtain.

Mrs. Wimple rushed through the backstage area, shooing everyone to their proper places. Then she patted her hair, and, just as the late bell for third period rang, stepped in front of the curtain.

"I'd like to welcome all of you to Howard Hoffer's first—and I hope annual—Salute to Shakespeare. Two of our eighth-grade classes have spent the term learning about his life and works . . ." She went on, but I was so nervous, I couldn't pay attention anymore.

What if I flubbed my lines? What if people laughed? What if I sounded stupid in front of everyone? Panic clamped my chest. I wanted to run. I reminded myself that it was just Shakespeare—someone I lived with every day, grew up hearing about. And KC and my friends thought I'd do okay. Gradually my chest loosened. My heart still pounded a heavy rhythm, but I no longer wanted to flee. Onstage, Mrs. Wimple kept going.

"I'd like to introduce two members of our community

who graciously agreed to help with our staged reading today. Using their expertise, they assisted in scene selections and pronunciation workshops, and have agreed to serve as our advisory board for next year's projects. Please welcome Drs. Penelope and Roger Kennedy."

Snickers and jeers came from the backstage shadows behind me. I started to feel the familiar burn of shame, but took a deep breath. They were Shakespeare-obsessed, but they were my parents.

Once onstage, my mother gave a deep curtsy to Mrs. Wimple, and Dad bowed. From the audience, I heard a few hoots, and then . . .

"Yeah, Professors K!"

"Whoo!"

"Huzzah!"

Clapping followed the cheering, which quickly spread to the rest of the audience. Then I realized—the older kids in the audience were my parents' students. Mom and Dad waved at the crowd, grinning from ear to ear as the applause continued. I made out some dim shapes standing beyond the stage, nearly out of the reach of the lights. They were giving my mom and dad a standing ovation—just for being introduced. The snickers behind me dried up.

Mom laughed and made a "quiet down" gesture with her hands. When the students settled, she took the microphone from Mrs. Wimple, who seemed rather bewildered at the display of attention.

"We are so glad you invited us to share your merry day," Mom said. "All the world's a stage, isn't it?" Her students hooted again. She passed the mic to Dad.

"'Tis a rare and noble undertaking which these young scholars hath accepted. And it is our privilege to participate in the endeavor's execution." They went on from there, speaking about the importance of the Globe Theatre and how happy they were to be involved with the event.

While they spoke, I noticed how happy they were and how much information they had. Call me crazy, but I'd never paid attention to that before, at home. I guess it's hard to notice things when you see them every day. It was obvious that they not only knew what they were talking about, but that they loved sharing it. They wanted us to get just as excited about Shakespeare as they were. And if it took dressing in costume or using the language to capture someone's attention and imagination, they'd do it.

Yeah, it was strange, but I was starting to "get" the strangeness a little more . . . maybe like they were starting to get me. KC was right—I needed to lighten up.

Next, Mom and Dad explained that their students had voted on the best Globes and scene stagings. Part of *their* grade would be to explain why when they returned to class at Chestnut next week.

They presented the award for best Globe Theatre to

partners Chrissy Li from my math class and Padma Anjou from the other language arts/social studies block. I was sure Ty would be disappointed, but he really couldn't expect that my parents would allow their students to pick our theater to win. Especially since Padma and Chrissy's featured hand-embroidered draperies and a working curtain. Mom and Dad even got the crowd to give a big Renaissance-era "huzzah!" for them when they got up onstage. Chrissy's ears were bright red, but both she and Padma wore oversized smiles on their faces. There was one on mine too.

When the other awards had been given—best scene staging, most creative—Mom and Dad took their seats in the audience and Mrs. Wimple came back to introduce the scenes.

"Before our *Midsummer Night's Dream* scenes begin, we'd like to have a more formal introduction of the writer who brought us all here together. Saber Greene and Mauri Lee will introduce the life of the Bard."

Applause swept across the audience again, and Saber and Mauri came out from the other curtain and stood in the center of the stage, each holding note cards. I held my breath, hoping our plan had worked.

"William Shakespeare was born in 1564, in Stratford-Upon-Avon, England," Saber read, staring intently at her card. Mrs. Wimple, standing just offstage, nodded.

"As a child, he enjoyed horseback riding and playing

the accordion," Mauri picked up, also reading directly off her card. A light murmur swept through the audience. I can't be sure, but I think it started where my parents' students were sitting.

"Once he grew up, he started writing plays, haiku, and limericks," Saber went on. Mrs. Wimple's forehead crinkled in confusion. Hissing whispers and gasps came from the group of Chestnut College students.

"His famous friends included Benjamin Franklin, Leonardo DaVinci, and Mozart," Mauri continued. With each piece of incorrect information, the atmosphere in the room turned even more cold and tense. Saber and Mauri were saying *exactly* what Dezzie had told them. They hadn't even double-checked to make sure that her information was accurate! A small part of me felt embarrassed for them—once they found out that nothing except Shakespeare's birthday was right, they were going to be mortified, furious, and not able to go on their trip—but the other, larger part of me remembered what they'd done to deserve it—ruined my father's favorite project, stole from my sister, and pretended to be her friend to get what they wanted. As the Bard never said, "Payback's a witch."

When they got to the part about Shakespeare having a working submarine built for rides up and down the Thames River, Mrs. Wimple coughed and a chuckle moved through the audience. Clearly unable to take it anymore,

Mrs. Wimple climbed the steps to the side of the stage and signaled to the girls that they were out of time. Still totally unaware of what just happened, Saber and Mauri stepped offstage. Principal Obin stood there, waiting for them. They were going to have a lot of explaining to do . . . and wouldn't be skiing this winter, I was sure.

Just before the principal led them away, I caught sight of Dezzie, waving at them. She'd taken off her tunic, and was wearing a Shakespeare tee all her own. Printed in big block letters on it were the words: "Though she be but little, she is fierce." Based on the expressions on Saber's and Mauri's faces, they didn't need Dezzie's help to understand what it meant.

Mrs. Wimple introduced the scene, and the other actors took their places. I was to wait in the wings until Puck's cue.

Nirmal, as Oberon, said, "How now, mad spirit! What night-rule now about this haunted grove?" He looked into the wings, straight at me.

For a second, I froze. What if I couldn't do it? What if they laughed? What if my parents laughed? Behind me, someone sneezed, snapping me out of my statued state. I took a deep breath and stepped onstage.

At first, the glare of Ty's lights made it hard to see. This was a good thing. I focused on Nirmal's face.

The words rolled in my mouth about as easily as triangular marbles. "My mistress . . . with a monster is . . . in love," I tried. I was near panic. I couldn't do it. I clunked through the next line. I touched my scarf, and I could stand a little straighter. I put my hand over the still-tingly spot on my cheek where KC kissed me, and something kicked in. My mother and father, KC, Ty, Ely, Judith, James, Dezzie, even Nirmal . . . they accepted this stand-out me. Maybe they *liked* this me. And maybe I could too.

Suddenly I felt like Puck, like a mischievous fairy, and the words flowed from me like Shakespeare himself was whispering them in my ear. "While she was in her dull and sleeping hour,/A crew of patches, rude mechanicals . . ." I finished the lines with a grin and a flourish, and glanced out at the audience.

My parents were front row, center, smiling wide and waving. Off to the side, I could see Dezzie's halo of curls and her proud expression. And then more faces popped out from the shadows—Judith, Ely, and even a flicker from the light booth and Ty.

And on the other side of the room, toward the back of the seats, two sneakers up in the air. KC, doing a hand-stand. I nearly broke character and laughed.

Offstage, scene over, I returned to my spot in the wings and waited for my heart to calm down. I tinkled one of the bells on my scarf, too soft for anyone to hear, and as I watched the story onstage unfold in front of me, I thought about the unexpected ways the start to this school year unfolded, as well. Anxiety provoking, annoying, and scary—yes. But also unique, creative, and distinctive. Maybe being anything but average wasn't a total tragedy after all.

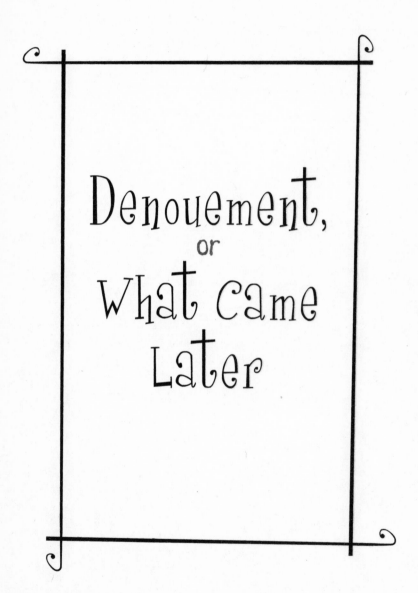

Denouement,
or
What came
Later

The Scene: *The Chilly Spoon, post–Salute to Shake-speare performance. The entire Kennedy family—still wearing their regalia/costume—around one table, KC, Ty, Ely, Judith and others fill the rest of the tables in the shop. Everyone happy, chatting, and eating ice cream.*

Dezzie (shielding her cup): Get your own!

Dad: I have my own, but it is a known fact that ice cream tastes better out of some-one else's cup.

Dezzie: Is that so, then?

In a quick motion, she stabs Dad's dessert and pops a heaping spoonful into her mouth. Everyone at the table is amazed by her speed and agility.

Dezzie (responding to their expressions): Fencing techniques.

Mom: I hereby declare a truce on all ice cream thievery, for we are here to celebrate Ham-let. *(directed to me)* You were a natural, honey.

Me (blushing): Thank you.

Dad: Shakespeare suits you. You were eloquent and impassioned.

Warmth spreads through me.

Dezzie: And you didn't even fumble your lines when Peaseblossom tripped in the second scene!

Me: Julie nearly took me down with her.

Dezzie hops onto her chair.

Dezzie: A toast! To Hamlet, whose mastery of the Bard shall lead her to greatness in the Kennedy clan!

She raises her empty cup. My parents and friends do the same.

All: Huzzah!

KC grins at me from across the room. I wrap my fingers around the paper cup next to my sundae, which contains an origami rose with a pig tucked inside, and smile back.

Me (in my best Elizabethan cheerleader voice): Huzzah!

I liked how it sounded.

ACKNOWLEDGMENTS

Writing this book required a full cast:

The Editor: Alisha Niehaus—who pushes, supports, and encourages me

The Agent: Sally Harding—who believes in my work and in me

The Cover Designer: Jeanine Henderson—for the beautiful cover

The Book Designer: Jasmin Rubero—for the beautiful interiors

The Copyeditor: Regina Castillo—who doesn't let me get away with anything

The Writing Group: Gary Crespo, Phoebe Sinclair, Megan Mullin, Ruthbea Clarke, Heather Hubbard, Annette Cinelli—who work as hard as I do on each of my novels

The Art History Expert: Dr. Kimberlee Cloutier-Blazzard— who made sure I knew my Pollock

The Ren Faire Expert: Kayte Bellusci—who helped me humiliate Hamlet even more

The Title Bestowers: Mandy Hubbard and Aprilynne Pike—who named *Total Tragedy*

The Support System: The 2009 Debutantes—who are always there for me

The Early Readers: Saundra Mitchell; Colleen, Chris, and Eliza Michaels—who gave their time to review the manuscript

The Artist: Judith Heiden Shimer—who gave her name to a character and created an amazing trailer for *Models Don't Eat Chocolate Cookies*

The Chorus: January O'Neil, Lauren Barnholdt, Scott & Dianne Simonini, and my friends and family—who cheer me on, every step of the way

The Husband: Frank—who loves me even when I'm writer-crazy

The Baby: CP—who has already given me new stories to tell

The Fans: Readers of *Models*—who let me know how much they liked that book

All of you have my deepest gratitude for the role you played in helping this story come to life. Thank you!